MICK MURPHY'S LAW

A Mick Murphy
Key West Mystery

MICHAEL HASKINS

Also by Michael Haskins

Chasin' the Wind – 2009
*Revenge – 2011
*Tijuana Weekend – 2011
Stairway to the Bottom – 2011
Free Range Institution – 2012
Car Wash Blues – 2013
To Beat the Devil – 2013
Nobody Wins – 2014

* Mick Murphy Mysteries not set in Key West

Dedication

For my sister Patty, thank you for the motivation, support and, most importantly, believing in me and being who you are.

Mick Murphy's Law
A Mick Murphy Key West Mystery

ISBN- 13: 978-1508403975
ISBN- 10: 150840397X

Trade Paperback
Published in 2015
Fenian Bastard Press

Michael Haskins
www.michaelhaskins.net

We are all in the gutter, but some of us are looking at the stars.

Oscar Wilde

The fear of death follows from the fear of life. A man who lives fully is prepared to die at any time.

Mark Twain

There is no hunting like the hunting of man, and those who have hunted armed men long enough and liked it, never care for anything else thereafter.

Ernest Hemingway

Began to Go Bad With a Call
Chapter ONE

No good comes from a phone call at three in the morning.

Kristofferson's *Shake Hands with the Devil,* the ringtone on my cellphone, woke me. The bedside clock radio displayed 3:07.

I sat up, unplugged the phone from its charger and saw **Richard** on the display screen. "Yeah?" I'd expected it to be someone needing bail money.

"Mick, get down to the hospital. Right now!" Key West Police Chief Richard Dowley's voice sounded stressed.

"What's happening?" I came fully awake, concerned because Richard didn't call at that hour.

"You know Robin Church." It rushed out as one, long word.

"Richard, what's going on?" I stood and slipped into my cargo shorts.

Robin and I had been friends since we met at a rodeo in Southern California, a long time ago. Briefly, we'd been lovers. A fling she'd called it. She liked the bad boys. I wasn't one. She rode out of my life with a bull rider in an old pickup. A few years ago, she arrived in Key West. We rekindled our friendship, that's all. Old habits die hard and before long she hooked up with a pimple-charmer named Morgan Pryce.

"She's asking for you," he said. "I'd hurry." He hung up.

I arrived at the emergency room entrance on the backside of the hospital on College Road in less than fifteen minutes. Richard hadn't told me to go the ER, but I knew. Two Key West Police cars were parked near the entrance and the officers waited inside the reception area.

In my head, I saw Robin from our California days. Young, long raven hair in a ponytail swaying across her back, faded jeans stuck into scruffy cowboy boots and a man's western shirt tied in a knot a little above her narrow waist. It somehow added to her sexy look, as she sauntered across the rodeo grounds missing piles of animal shit that others seemed not to. Cowboys turned to watch her. I did, too.

Officer Billy Wardlow walked me past the nurses' station and into the ER. Richard stood in front of a draped off area talking to a doctor. He looked up as I walked in and excused himself.

"I'm sorry, Mick," he said quietly. "She's been asking for you."

"What happened?" The septic smell of the ER always bothered me. The quiet hum of machines, the loud pleads for help from patients and family mixed in a cacophony of sound that stayed with me for days.

"You knew she was pregnant?" He avoided my question by asking his own.

I nodded. "Something gone wrong?" He said, *was pregnant.*

Richard looked down at the floor and then at the doctor and nurse talking across from us.

"Morgan beat her." I'd never heard Richard's voice quiver before. "You'd better talk to her. It's not good."

He pulled aside the curtain and I went in. The curtain closed. Overhead, artificial light cast shadows in the sterile area.

I wouldn't have recognized the person lying in the bed as Robin. Monitors beeped above her, lines from medicine packets on an IV stand ran to needles stuck into her arm. Tape kept them in place.

Swollen, black, blue and red welts hid her sapphire eyes. A nose once straight as a ruler, lay bent and flat against her gray skin. The shock stopped me for a moment. This wasn't Robin. There'd been a mistake. Ashamed of myself, I walked next to her and reached for her hand.

She moved. I looked toward the monitors, but no alarm went off. I stroked her hand. Something much stronger than anger turned in my stomach and I realized tears seeped from my eyes.

"Mick?" My name fumbled out of her broken lips.

I bent down and kissed her forehead. "I'm here, Robin."

"Baby girl." Her words came softly, in unnatural, multiple syllables.

I bent closer.

Robin's head turned toward me. Her eyes couldn't open and a soft wince came as I saw the welts over them stirred slightly. A tear from my cheek fell onto her face. I wiped it away, feeling the heat from her battered face.

"Take ... care ... of ... my ... baby." Again, the words came out broken and hard to understand.

I nodded, then realized she couldn't see. "I will," I whispered into her ear. "Until you get better."

A nurse pulled the curtain aside and motioned for me to join Richard.

I kissed her forehead and lightly squeezed her hand. "I'm right outside, Robin." I wiped my eyes as I left the room.

"They took the baby?" I said to the nurse.

She looked at Richard.

"The baby didn't make it, Mick." His voice soft and sad, very unlike him. "They didn't want to tell her."

"Why isn't she in ICU?" My words sounded harsh, even to me.

Richard motioned a doctor over. He stood six foot and looked skinny under his white smock. His black skin shiny from sweat, even though the room felt chilly.

"We tried to save the baby," the doctor said as he looked at the papers on his clipboard. "We couldn't. The child was already dead."

He paused and looked at more papers. "This is unusual,"

he said, and I guessed he meant talking to me. "Because it's a criminal case, I can give you the details. You're Murphy?" He glanced at me.

I nodded.

"Mr. Murphy the patient asked for you upon arrival," he read from the clipboard. "Chief Dowley said he'd contact you and we took the patient to the OR for a cesarean procedure."

"Her name is Robin Church!" Anger, hurt and helplessness built inside and the pressure pounded in my head.

"I'm sorry," the doctor said.

Richard grabbed my arm. "Let the doctor do his job, Mick. No one likes this."

"Bottom line, Mr. Murphy, is Robin wasn't expected to live through the cesarean. We tried to save the baby. Whoever beat her left Robin with massive internal bleeding, a damaged kidney, liver, broken ribs that tore into her lungs and we have no idea of what damage has occurred in her . . . I mean, Robin's brain. I can only say that Robin's will to live until you got here kept her alive."

"She talked to me! She told me about a baby girl."

"Yes." The doctor looked toward Richard. "I thought it best to keep the news from her. We are making her . . . Robin as comfortable as possible."

I turned to Richard. "You know Morgan did this?"

"We have the first responders and two officers that asked her who did this and Robin said Morgan," Richard said. "The crime lab people are at her house, there'll be other evidence, too. We've got a BOLO on him and the sheriff has it. He won't get out of the Keys, Mick."

"Have you been to the club?"

"Detectives and officers are there now. They're interviewing the strippers and staff and going through his office. We'll get him."

I turned to the doctor. "Can I sit with Robin?"

"Of course," he said. "When the time comes . . ."

"I'll leave, doctor."

He forced a smile. "There was little we could do. We've made her as comfortable as possible and she isn't feeling any pain."

"Thank you doctor," I said.

"It's only a matter of time, Mick, before we've got Morgan." Richard opened the curtain for me.

"Hope so," I said. "Because when I leave here, I'm going looking for him too."

I pulled a chair over to the bed, sat down and took Robin's hand in mine. In my head, I tried to remember the fun we had in California and even being on the water in Key West, but my eyes couldn't move from Robin's battered face, and whatever it was that stirred inside me grew angrier and pounded in my head.

Promise Made
Chapter TWO

When Robin's heart monitor straight-lined, I kissed her good-by and let go of her hand. It was still warm. Nurses began to enter the room and asked me to leave. Of course, they had patients' monitors at the nurses' station. They could read the changing numbers and knew what they meant and what was about to happen, before I did.

The doctor came in and shook his head as he went to verify his prediction.

I left hoping Robin somehow sensed I stayed until the end. Having made her a promise, I'd said all I had to say. I wiped my eyes and didn't look back.

Richard had gone. Other nurses and doctors rushed about and read clipboards of information as patients moaned from behind curtained-off rooms.

My head pounded but the medicine I needed couldn't be found in the ER.

Outside, the sun had come up. How could the day look so perfect? Maybe the universe didn't care about Robin as I did. It probably didn't care about any of us and that's why the sun comes up each morning. I looked at my wristwatch. It was a few minutes past eight. Five hours ago, my life began to shatter because of a phone call. It only got worse from there. For a person who couldn't remember crying too often since childhood, my tear ducts were on overdrive. There had been things in my life that should've made me cry, but hadn't. I didn't understand the effect Robin's death held over me. I'd lost control of a part of me and that feeling was new.

I stood beside my old white Jeep and had no idea of what to do next. Cars moved along College Road, hidden from sight by shrubbery, but I could hear them. Florida Keys Community College had its Key West campus around the bend, across from the hospital's main entrance. Further on, the Monroe County jail and sheriff's office dwelled next to the Gulf of Mexico.

I asked, *Why Robin*, to a God I wasn't sure listened or cared. I asked myself why smart women get mixed up with abusive men. Why do they stay in the relationship? I did know that abusive people were bullies and cowards, man or woman. In most cases, they were no better than rabid animals.

I stood by the Jeep repeating *rabid animals* to myself.

Would the police have changed the BOLO to be on the lookout for a murder suspect? I should have asked Richard if the charge would be two murders because of the baby.

For one last time, I wiped my eyes on a dirty rag from the backseat of the Jeep, and knew I needed to go to the Silver Slipper Saloon, the strip club on Duval Street that Morgan managed.

Early Saturday morning and Duval Street had little traffic. I expected to see police cars outside the club, but didn't. Could the police have interviewed the club's strippers and staff already? Using my Jeep's emergency flashers, I pulled over and parked.

As I thought about it, I realized the questioning of people at the club would be for information on where Morgan could've gone, nothing else. I crossed the street and checked the door. It was locked. I looked through the glass panel and only the security lights in back were on. I banged on the door. I banged again. I looked down the side alley where I knew the strippers had an entrance. No one came out. I ran down the alley and banged on the side door harder than necessary. No one came. The solid-wood door had no window to look through.

Officer Julio Avael leaned against my Jeep, the red and blue lights of his police car flashing. I walked across the street.

"Julio," I said as I approached.

"We were done in there more than an hour ago," he said.

"We'll get Morgan. Didn't know the woman, but all the cops know him. We're called here enough."

"The sooner the better." I shut off the Jeep's emergency flashers.

"The Chief wants to see you," Julio said. "He thought you might be here, eventually."

"He's at the station?" I got in the Jeep and wondered what Richard wanted. "Why didn't he call?"

"You don't answer your cell," he said.

I checked my phone and it was off. When I entered the ER, I must have shut it off, but I didn't remember. I turned it on and listened to Richard's first message.

"Harpoon Harry's?" I said.

"He needs his *con leche*, we called him at one-thirty this morning," Julio said. "The responding officers and medics knew it was bad, Mick. You know the unwritten rule is you don't kill a police officer, pregnant woman or child. We solve those cases, no matter how long it takes. This shit doesn't happen in Key West."

"I hope you find him, Julio." I drove to Harpoon Harry's. Breakfast was not my priority.

Richard's unmarked police car took up part of the loading zone. I pulled in behind it.

Ron Heck, the owner, handed me a large *café con leche,* an espresso and steamed milk, and pointed toward the back of the diner. "Richard said you'd want this. Three sugars."

I took the cup and found Richard in the back, alone. I sat down.

"What were you going to do at the club?" He wasn't smiling.

"I thought the girls would talk to me."

Kathy took our order. I realized no one had heard about Robin. Her death had happened too early, but the news might make Bill Becker's radio broadcast Monday morning. Then again, it might not. It depended on what Richard wanted to release and when.

"We already talked to them."

"Yeah, but you're cops. They might say something to me they wouldn't want to say to you."

"They're not involved." Richard finished his *con leche*.

"No," I said, "but they might know where Morgan's gone. Or have an idea."

"And if they did, you'd call, right?" He looked at me hard like a cop, not a friend.

"Definitely," I lied and he knew it. "Is it two murders?"

"Catherine is writing up the arrest warrant for the judge," he said. "But the final decision is hers, when it comes to trail."

Catherine Vogel is the State Attorney in Key West for the Florida16[th] Judicial Circuit.

"You have her working on Saturday?"

"I briefed her on the phone and a detective is meeting her to go over the evidence we've got," he said. "We have enough for a warrant and she's going to make sure it's done right. We don't want evidence tossed because of the way the warrant is written."

Our breakfast came and we ate slowly, without talking.

"I don't want you going after Morgan." Richard said when Kathy took our plates.

"I don't want to either," I said. "So get him."

Richard smiled, but it was not a happy one. "FDLE has the BOLO, so Morgan won't get out of Florida, if he somehow gets off the Keys."

Florida Department of Law Enforcement is a state police agency.

"Why am I here?"

"I probably should know better, but I thought if you knew what we're doing, you might stay out of it," he said.

I waited quietly.

"Okay," Richard said. "Robin's car is at home, so Morgan is on his motorcycle or someone's driving him. We've got his DMV photo with all law enforcement between here and the bordering states. His license indicates he's six-four, two-hundred and eighty-five pounds. He can't hide, he's big as a horse."

"He could be holed up in the Keys," I said. "Waiting."

"A possibility, but he's only delaying capture, because when he goes to leave, we've got him. We also checked the morning flights, and he wasn't on one," Richard recited what his department had done. "No one his size bought a ticket this morning and there were only a couple of early morning flights."

"Private plane, boat," I said.

"No private planes flew out before sunrise," he said. "Boat's a possibility but the Marine Patrol has the BOLO and is hitting the Florida marinas as best they can."

"Sounds like you've got it covered," I said. "Will you call me when you get him?"

"As soon as I know, you're the first person I'll call. Promise. Now make me a promise."

It was my turn to try a tired smile. "Anything."

"Go home, get some sleep and wait for my call," he said in his cop's voice. "It's coming."

"Good advice," I said. "I am tired."

"Stay away from the Silver Slipper."

"Haven't been inside since Chuck left as the manager. No reason to go inside now," I continued to lie.

Richard watched as I left and his calloused look assured me he knew I lied.

The Silver Slipper
Chapter THREE

It wasn't all lies I'd told Richard. I did go home and sleep, but it was restless. I woke at two in the afternoon, anxious and weary. A few aspirins didn't help my headache either. My phone hadn't chirped. Richard hadn't caught Morgan in the four hours since I left him. Even with traffic, Morgan could've been out of the Keys in less time.

I grabbed a cigar from the humidor, went out to the back porch, sat down and lit it. Wispy white clouds blew across an ocean-blue sky, bright with sunshine. Another perfect day in Key West. More proof we didn't matter in the big picture of the universe. Looking toward the gazebo, I thought of nothing and everything.

The cigar should have relaxed me more than it did, but the anger burning inside me began to get my mind racing with the old *what ifs* I had dealt with as a journalist.

I couldn't discover what led to Robin's death unless I got to Morgan. I knew he had been abusive, a bully who used his size and strength to belittle others, to scare and intimidate them. There had to be something I could get hold of that would lead me to him.

Johnny Bishop, my old editor on the Record-American once told me, after I made no headway trying to interview a politician in a scandal, *When they slam the door in your face, look for an unlocked window.* Maybe the strippers were Morgan's unlocked window. All of them were smaller than he was, plied their trade for cash and were ripe for the picking, if the picker was the size of a Clydesdale and had the brain of a goldfish. Would he pass up free money he could extort from the girls with just a growl? I doubted it.

When they knew he wasn't coming back, couldn't hurt them, maybe there were things they'd share with me that they wouldn't with a cop. Maybe it was worth checking out.

The unfinished cigar went into the ashtray. I needed to get to the Silver Slipper Saloon. It didn't open until 8 PM, but I knew the bar staff showed up around three and the girls soon after.

Dixie, an older southern belle, really ran the day-to-day operations of the saloon, leaving Morgan time to throw his weight around and show the club's bouncers how to do their job. Of course, Morgan took the credit for many of Dixie's decisions. She'd be a good person to start with.

I found a parking spot on Simonton Street, paid four dollars into the theft-machine for two hours, and walked through the crowded blocks to the Silver Slipper. The Duval Street door remained locked. I walked around to the off-street entrance, a glass door that the bar backs and other employees used.

Inside the lights were dim. When the girls were on stage, gyrating for customers, bright lights highlighted their movements, glistening off their sweating bodies, while the rest of the club hid in shadows.

"We're closed," a guy behind the bar said as he dumped a large bucket of ice into the beer cooler.

"I'm looking for Dixie," I said.

"You are?" He looked up, didn't recognize me and waited.

"Mick Murphy, she knows me."

He walked away, heading in back, without saying anything.

Dixie, and I doubted that was her real name, danced in the club when it wasn't much more than a slapped together shack. She draped herself in the Confederate battle flag on stage at first and when she was done you'd forgotten about the flag and wondered how the South lost the war. Of course, you questioned it while stuffing dollar bills or maybe five-dollar bills into her garter. By that point, that's all she wore.

The girls got younger, Dixie didn't. She talked herself into a job behind the bar. When the whole building went through remodeling, she came out as the bar manager. I wouldn't dare guess her age, or ask it, but dressed, she has a better-looking body than most of the girls on stage. I guess that's the difference between a girl and a woman. Girls who keep it together carry their beauty into womanhood. Dixie still turned heads, even while naked girls twirled on stage.

"Mick Murphy, darlin'!" Dixie yelled my name in her southern drawl as she pushed through the black curtain of the lap-dance area. Still only five-foot-five, her bleach-blonde hair not long enough for her once trademark ponytail, and cold, gray eyes that looked through you. "You don't remember what time we open?" She laughed and we hugged. "Been a long time."

"Chuck was a friend," I said as she pulled away. "Morgan . . ."

"Is a pig!" She barked. "I hope pig farmers can forgive me. Y'all haven't joined the police department, have you?"

"No."

"You know they came here at closing this morning."

"Yeah."

"Oh God!" Her face went blank. "You know the woman. I'm sorry, Mick, darlin'."

"Yeah. I've known her for a long time." The cops hadn't told Dixie and the girls why there were looking for Morgan, or that Robin had died, but she guessed well.

There was an awkward moment of silence and it took on a surreal feel as I looked around the room that is usually full of loud music, bellowing men and naked women.

"What can you tell me about Morgan that maybe you forgot to tell the cops?" I broke the uneasiness and watched relief cross her face.

"We all talked about it after the cops left," she said and sat on a barstool. "Thing is, none of the girls like him. You know about the Russians, right?"

"Only rumors."

"I think you can tell when a rumor is mostly fact."

"Okay. The Russian or some other Eastern European gang supplies the girls."

"Most of them, darlin'. They either come here close to a virgin as you can get or as seasoned pros," she said. "I think it's the pros' job to break in the inexperienced. I'm being kind."

"I thought so."

"Morgan, of course, always found one of the new girls to break in." Her lips turned into a scowl and she wiped her mouth with the back of her hand. "Nothing you could do about it." I think she said it more for her comfort than my education.

"About two years ago, a couple of Russians came here," she said. "I thought maybe the girls had complained about him. But by the end of the night they were kissin' cousins they were so friendly."

"What happened?"

She twisted around on the barstool. She smiled and frowned, making up her mind on what to tell me or at least how much.

"I didn't know her," she said of Robin. "He wouldn't let her come here. Sometimes in bad weather she'd drive him and I'd see her drop him off. I guess he was afraid to get his Harley wet. I'd see her and even talked to her once in Winn-Dixie. But I didn't really know her."

"The point, Dixie," I said.

"He hoarded money, darlin'," she said and stopped twisting on the barstool. "He extorted money every night from the girls. Even the Russian girls."

"I figured that. He leave the bar alone?"

She chuckled. "The old man would've had Chuck break his arms and legs if he touched the till, liquor or the door."

"How much could he get from the girls?"

"A few hundred a week night, more on the weekend," she said. "Interesting that the Russians didn't care."

"They don't take to skimming very kindly," I said. "There a reason they didn't kill him?"

"Oh sure, darlin'," she said. "They gave him the chump change because he came through for them when they asked him to. They had him up in Miami for a week and after he came back things changed. The Russians came here once a month. Morgan and them worked on something one week upstairs after we closed. All kind of secret goin' ons. Know what I mean?"

"No," I said and wondered if these Russians were part of Alexei's cartel. The elusive Alexei I had been trying to locate and kill for the past two years because his men murdered my fiancée Tita, sank my sailboat and almost killed me.

"You wouldn't believe me, Mick." Dixie stood. "I didn't believe it when one of the girls mentioned what she had to do. Then after everyone went home, I saw for myself."

"Saw what?"

She took my hand. "See for yourself." She pulled me into the lap-dance room.

Mirrors, Mirrors, Mirrors
Chapter FOUR

When Dixie walked me through the black curtain into the lap-dance room, the brightness surprised me. Eight curtained-off areas, four on either side of the walkway, featured a large chair where the client sat and the girl mounted him for the lap dance. There was just enough room for three, in case the client brought his wife or girlfriend along, or if he had enough credit on his gold card to pay for two strippers and a bottle of champagne.

Black painted ceiling, floor and walls made it the perfect darkroom, feigning privacy. At night, when strippers took customers back here, the only lights on were red, low-wattage bulbs and the curtains were drawn. Anger grew inside me when I found myself comparing it to the curtained-off room where Robin had died a few hours ago. Dixie saw my surprise but misconstrued it.

"Need to see to clean, darlin'," she said, still holding my hand. "Condoms, business cards with phone numbers scribbled on the back. You wouldn't believe what we find when we clean. Dirty towels the girls use to catch and clean . . . well, you know."

"I don't smell disinfectant," I said.

"Soap and hot water."

Water, anyway, I thought, because I knew the old man who owned the saloon could be tight with his money. *Bring it in*, he once told me, *not send it out.*

She pulled me along and at the back of the room, she let go of my hand and used a key to open a door. A stairway led to the second floor, an area set aside for storage, or so I thought. Dixie switched on the overhead red light.

"Careful," she said and walked slowly up the narrow stairway.

Another light switch at the top and diffused lights turned on in the hallway that ran the length of the club. "What are you showing me?" The area gave me a bad feeling, something I often felt during my journalist's day in Mexico, covering the drug war. I listened to the feeling then and I was about to turn around and go back downstairs.

"I told you Morgan liked to make a new girl his project," Dixie said, her words filled with malice. "His little love shack is up here."

"I don't care about his shacking up," I said, still nervous. "I want to know where he is."

As soon as the words were out of my mouth, I grabbed Dixie and turned her to me.

"He's up here?" I whispered.

"Darlin', he'd been up here we all would've turned him in. What's up here is why the Russian mob lets him extort money from the girls."

Unlike the lap-dance room, the walls here were pink, the doors red and a soft light burned above each one. The floor had thick carpet and the opposite wall had pink, red and white sheer fabric strung in loops along it. In a western movie, this would have been the whorehouse.

"Kind of fancy for storage," I said, fighting my unease.

"A couple of small dorms for the Russian girls. I guess Morgan might call that storage." Dixie stopped at the second door from the stairway. "This isn't one of them, darlin'." She took another key and unlocked the door. "I bet you never seen anything like this before." She opened the door.

In each corner of the room's ceiling, red lights shone. A large king-sized bed took up much of the space, covered with all sizes of pillows that almost hid black, silk sheets. As my eyes adjusted to the light, I realized my vision hadn't been off because of the light, but because the lights reflected from mirrors that replicated everything in the room, a number of times over; including us. Full-length mirrors covered the ceiling and all four walls. Even the inside door had a mirror covering it.

Dixie closed the door and our reflections multiplied themselves on the ceiling and walls. Unable to stop myself, I looked down at the floor, expecting mirrors, and saw thick black carpet.

"This is a love nest?" I felt uncomfortable being in the room. "It looks like the circus hall of mirrors."

"This is a money maker." With a small pillow in her hand, Dixie walked to the mirrored wall nearest the foot of the bed. "Come here."

I walked over, watching my multiple images along the walls.

Dixie pressed the pillow against a panel and pushed. It opened slightly and she slipped her fingers behind the panel and pried it open. She walked in, hit a light switch and muted lights came on.

"Took me a while to find my way in here," she said.

What came next totally surprised me.

Maybe the size of a medium walk-in closet the room held ten mounted computer monitors or flat screen TVs, I wasn't sure. Each hooked up to its own DVD recorder stored in racks off to the side and a director's control board like you'd see on MSNBC's Morning Joe when they show the control room. The director's panel faced the room we just left. The big surprise, as if I hadn't seen enough, came when I turned toward the control panel and looked into the other room. Two-way mirrors on the wall.

A chair rested in front of the control panel and I sat down. "What the hell is this?"

"You know what this is, darlin'." Dixie opened her arms and swept the room as she turned.

"Tell me," I said.

Dixie stopped turning. She leaned against the wall opposite me. "Each monitor is hooked to a camera in the other room. Ten cameras, just about covers every angle you would need for recording a porno."

"Blackmail?" I don't know why I sounded surprised.

Dixie nodded. "The Russians arrange it and Morgan makes it happen. He's the director."

"Who the hell you gonna black mail in Key West?"

"Locally, you have the military." She sat on the arm of the chair. "Key West is a destination, darlin', and the Russians keep track of certain people, maybe even help them come here. They're always men. Give 'em a few too many drinks at bars along Duval and they end up here. Morgan's waiting for them. A friendly girl, a free lap dance, the discussion goes in the direction of the guy wants more."

"And they end up here."

"More often than you could guess."

"And you're involved how?"

"I'm not, officially. One of the new girls told me about the room. She thought I knew," Dixie said. "I had the key for the stairway because of the dorm situation. It didn't take me long to find Morgan's extra key for the door and to make a copy. I didn't know about this room or the scheme. Morgan doesn't know I know."

"Why show me? You going to stop it?"

"Darlin', in all the years you've known me, have I ever taught Sunday school?"

"So why?"

"Money." The cold way she said the word and the smile that formed on her lips afterward, told me all I needed to know. She planned to replace Morgan.

"So, why show all this to me?"

"I want Morgan caught," she said and stroked my beard. "You hate him, you have a reason to kill him."

"The police will catch him, not me." I didn't sound convincing.

"You're looking for him and I wanted to show you this

because when you get close, you need to remember that just because you can't see him, doesn't mean he ain't there."

Questions and Answers
Chapter FIVE

Morgan couldn't hide in plain sight, he was too big and clumsy. But I understood Dixie's warning. He could be deceptive, as well as threatening. I hadn't thought of that. It occurred to me that I hadn't thought anything through to its conclusion. *What ifs*, carried to the end always took into consideration negative as well as positive outcomes. The local cops had closed the door to my involvement, but I found Dixie to be a wide-open window of opportunity. Silently, I thanked Johnny Bishop for taking me under his wing in the old Boston city room.

Looking around, I noticed empty racks. "DVD storage?" I pointed at them.

"This is all assumption on my part, Mick darlin'." Dixie stood and walked to the racks. "Morgan would take the recording from each of the cameras, find what he wanted and edit it all together for the Russians on one DVD. These racks held the raw footage."

"He came back for them?" Seemed risky for someone who knew he had to get out of Dodge and quickly. "Or for the originals?"

She removed a rack from the wall and slid a panel aside. "He came back for this." Using another key, she opened a small, concealed wall safe. "He came back for the money, wads of money." Opening the safe's door, she pointed at the empty compartment. "The Russians must've got the originals or he kept them somewhere else, but I never saw them. He took the raw stock DVDs, too."

"A lot of hiding places." I didn't need to be concerned about the missing DVDs, they weren't of interest. "How come you know about them?"

"I know because when the girl told me of taking a

customer up here on Morgan's orders, I became curious."
She left the safe open and sat back on the arm of the chair.
"He kept extra sets of everything, especially keys, because
he misplaced them all the time. Can't run this place without
keys."

"So it seems."

"I found a set in his office, had copies made for that
room," she pointed through the two-way mirror. "Once I
found this room here, I went looking for his other hidey-
holes."

"He has a lot of 'em?" It really wasn't a question.

"Is the pope catholic?" She giggled like a schoolgirl,
something she must have practiced when she had her nights
on the mirrored stage downstairs and never forgot. Nothing
like a teenage squeal to excite the customers. "He trusted no
one."

"Rightfully so." I nodded toward the open safe. "You
watched the DVDs."

"You think, darlin'? Never saw a final cut, but saw a lot
of flesh from in there." She indicated the pillow-covered bed.
"Surprising thing was the quality."

"Surprising in what way?"

"I had a small part in a few flicks, back in the late '90s,"
she said. "Needed the money. They were pros and the quality
wasn't as good as what I saw up here, and Morgan's no pro.
The Russians must've taught him how to do it."

In the '90s, her looks would've been youthful and
alluring, so I wondered if her movie roles where small or did
she have her deceptive side, too. Don't we all? I sat there
deceiving her, acting as if I cared about her frivolous world,
but led her on, hoping to find out more about Morgan and
maybe it would eventually lead me to him.

"Did you recognize anyone?" I tried making sense of a
blackmail scheme in Key West. Maybe the military was the
target.

"A few repeat customers." Dixie stood, closed the safe and put the empty rack back in place. "Do you think the cops'll do a thorough search?"

"Don't know." I wanted to know about the repeat customers. "Repeat customers up here or downstairs?"

"Downstairs." She leaned against the mirrored glass. "There was a difference between the footage I watched and real porn."

"You said the quality. What else?"

"Of course, the angles were more drastic, wider shots than in porn. You didn't see penetration. Knew it was happening, but no close-up camera shots."

"Quality and camera shots, that it?" I didn't want a lesson on shooting porn.

"No, the script was off," she said. "The girl is always asking the john questions, 'I'm better than your wife,' or she's giving head and asks, 'Your wife doesn't do this?' or maybe, 'Your secretary and wife aren't as good as me.' Stuff like that."

"Something the john wouldn't want his wife to hear," I said. "Or see on the Internet."

"Exactly, the perfect blackmail video," she said. "If it was the first time the john had ever been with a hooker, it didn't matter, he still couldn't deny what he said."

"The johns were drunk, or maybe drugged."

"Morgan had the drugs available, that's for sure," Dixie said. "But with men, booze is usually all that's needed and maybe a little encouragement from the guys he's with."

"The men you saw," I pointed through the mirror into the next room, "they weren't locals? No city or county politicians?"

"No." She shook her head. "Morgan ain't smart enough to do any of this on his own. My guess would be the Russians set the whole thing up. They'd give Morgan a call, he prepares the girl and sets the encounter up. Some of the footage was kind of kinky too."

"Morgan's got money and we assume some original DVDs, before he took off, right?" I tried to think of what could be next for him.

"Money for sure," Dixie said. "You trying to figure out what he did when he left the club?"

"It would help."

"Called the Russians?" she said.

If he were that stupid, we'd never see him again. "He's on the lam, he's lost his usefulness to them," I said. "The only help they'd give him is a watery grave."

"We can only hope." Dixie smiled. "If anyone deserves it . . ."

"Who else would he call?" I cut her off; I needed her thinking survival.

"His old motorcycle gang," she said.

That surprised me. I'd never heard talk of Morgan and a motorcycle gang. I knew some rough types filled the club in September during the annual Poker Run, but always thought of him as a wanna be.

"And they are?"

"No idea of the gang's name," she said. "He often bragged and showed off his biker tats. Thought it might impress or at least scare us because he was so bad."

"Anything else you can remember?" The noise below warned me the girls were in the bar with the staff. I wanted to make sure Dixie told me all she knew before we locked up and went back downstairs.

"He bragged about terrorizing Panama City whenever the gang went there," she said. "But I don't know if I believe him."

"Why wouldn't you believe him?"

"Tourist town, military town, the cops wouldn't put up with it," she said. "But other places in the Panhandle, they might."

Even with the thick carpet and mirrored walls, I heard soft voices go by outside.

"The Russian girls," Dixie said. I guess she saw my concern. "There might be something. When he was showing off his tats, he had one of a rattlesnake on his upper arm."

I didn't say anything. If the snake had a meaning, she'd tell me.

"You ever hear of the Rattlers?"

I shook my head.

"A motorcycle gang in the Panhandle, Alabama and Louisiana, too," she said. "Maybe that was the gang he was in."

"Maybe, Dixie. Thanks." I stood up. "You know one thing, for sure, the Russians know."

"About Morgan?"

I pointed toward the wall. "At least one of them girls knows who to call. After the cops talked to them, she called the boss."

"Maybe I should get the number and call, too," she said. "We'd better get out of here."

"Dixie, my advice is to stay clear of the Russians. They may want to make this whole operation go away and you don't need to be a loose end."

"If it was profitable, they'd want to keep it going." She smiled.

"Literally, Dixie darlin'," I mimicked her drawl, "you'd be putting your life on the line."

Norm and Friends
Chapter SIX

I left the Silver Slipper and turned toward the Smokin' Tuna Saloon, only a couple of blocks away. The late afternoon sun had already begun to set. The days grew shorter and it would be dark by happy hour. Early darkness, since we turned the clock back an hour a week ago. Winter months depressed me with the lack of sunshine. I preferred the spring when the days attacked the darkness and eked out a little more daylight, one day at a time. Summer sunsets after 8 PM were perfect.

Bartenders and servers from other saloons sat around the main bar, off from their day shifts, using the quiet of the Tuna before happy hour and live music as a place to socialize. Alain, the pony-tailed bartender from Canada waited on customers.

I sat at the Bamboo Bar as the happy hour bartenders set it up for opening, away from the crowd, and didn't really want a drink. No, that's not true. I wanted a lot to drink. Maybe it would help me forget, but right at that moment I didn't want to forget about Robin.

I wanted to get my hands on Morgan Pryce and do what, I hadn't even thought of it yet. Dixie's information about the Russian mob being involved with him rekindled another flame of hatred I'd not extinguished. If what she said was true, then Morgan had been working for Alexei's men out of Miami. And while I wanted Morgan badly, I'd chased Alexei for a long time so I could put a bullet between his eyes.

Dixie's information rattled around in my head. Rattlesnake tats were also there. If Morgan had an affiliation with the Rattlers Motorcycle Gang, he'd be safer with its members than with the Russians. Would he be smart enough to know that? It was a starting point and I doubted the police had gotten the information from Dixie.

Going to the Panhandle and separating Morgan from the Rattlers would be a dangerous challenge. One I couldn't face by myself. Bob, Pauly and Burt were here and dependable. The four of us would be shorthanded confronting the Rattlers, so we'd have to use brains over brawn. That almost made me laugh aloud. It's not often, if ever, the four of us were thought of as a brain trust.

When, and if, I knew for sure Alexei's crime syndicate was involved, I would have to reach out to Norm. He might be only one man, but the five of us would be a force to reckon with, be it bikers, Russian gangsters or any mixture thereof. Norm, an elusive government black-bag specialist that I've come to assume works out of JSOC, Joint Special Operations Command, and I go back to my journalist days in Southern California, Central America and Mexico. Opposites attract and we are at different ends of the political stick. Our friendship lasts only because we know when we lie to each other and why.

My head began to ache like yesterday's long hangover when my cell threw out Kristofferson's voice. I looked twice, but the readout showed **Norm** each time.

"Just thinking 'bout you." I hoped my voice hid my anxiety. It wasn't the right time to bring him up to date on Robin's murder or that there could be a connection to Alexei.

"Talkin' 'bout you for the last hour, hoss." Norm sounded beat and the background noise made him hard to hear.

"You at an airport somewhere?"

"Hell, no, I'm in Key West!"

I'd dealt with enough surprises in the last twelve hours. I didn't need this one.

"Why?" I should've shown more enthusiasm but I knew Norm's being anywhere meant trouble.

"Remember the Irish sisters we met in California?" His voice was suddenly energized.

"No," I said. My mind raced back to earlier this year as my search for Cousin Cecil had led me to Southern California, some old stomping grounds, Norm and, as usual, trouble.

"From McGinty's," Norm said as a reminder. "You remember McGinty's and your IRA friends."

"Norm, all I remember about those two days is British bastards wanting to torture me and none of 'em were sisters," I said.

"Nora, Brigid, Peggy and Seanan Naughton." He wanted me to remember.

"Their father owns a pub somewhere?" It wasn't clear, but the memory was there.

"In Fort Lauderdale. See, you remember."

"I thought you were here."

"I am. We are."

"We?" I didn't need this craziness.

"I'm with Nora and Peggy." He lowered his voice and I barely heard him. "We're at Schooner Wharf. Some fuckin' idiot's revving his boat's engines and I can't hear myself think."

I didn't answer. My thoughts raced and an idea began to form. Maybe Norm was a Godsend? Maybe.

"You there, hoss?" He spoke more clearly.

"Yeah, yeah. Let me ask you something."

"Meet us over here and ask me anything."

"Let me ask and you can work on an answer while I walk over."

"Shoot."

"You've got the ability to find me anywhere, right?"

"Not that hard, Mick. Why?"

"Suppose I needed your help in finding someone. Could you do it?"

"What are the cops for?" Now he sounded suspicious.

"Not the question I asked."

"I've got my ways. Who is it?"

I gave him Morgan's name and his possible association with the Rattlers, and that he was a fugitive, but left out what he did.

"What's he wanted for?" Norm's curiosity was piqued.

"Assault," I lied, "but it could end up being murder."

"Whose toes am I gonna step on?"

"Local and state," I said. "But if they don't know . . ."

"I can try to locate him," Norm said over the background noise, "but can't control where the information ends up."

"That's okay."

"What happens when you know where he is?" Norm's curiosity turned to caution.

"Depends.

"On what?"

I hesitated because I hadn't thought it through and his question was another reminder of that. What did I plan to do? "There's a chance he's connected to Alexei."

Silence, well the engine in the background still roared, but Norm said nothing at first.

"How long will it take you to get here?" he said. "We need to talk about all of it."

I Want the Son-of-a-Bitch
Chapter SEVEN

Past the two hours of parking I'd paid for and the old Jeep had avoided a ticket. In Key West, that's like drawing to an inside royal straight flush. Not wanting to push my luck with the city's parking enforcement, I drove to Schooner Wharf Bar. On Margaret Street, I found an empty spot and took it. Two small things like no parking ticket and finding a free residential parking spot and I knew my day had improved. Things were looking up and then I remembered Norm. And the sisters!

Why did he bring two colleens who worked the family's Irish pub in Fort Lauderdale, to Key West? He had to be up to something but I couldn't make sense of it. Norm's particular skills took him out of the country. He hated the tropics. His ideal vacation locale had cool summers and mountains, not a steamy island. More than once he'd said he hated Key West. If he wanted free-range chickens running around the streets and humidity, he'd go the Central America or the Mexican countryside.

Thinking about Norm and his reasons for being in Key West actually got my mind away from the existing problem. Robin no longer had problems. Sorry as I was, and as much as I wished I'd done something more to help her, I couldn't undo the past.

However, I could keep the promises I made to her in the ER and settle scores with Morgan. For that, I needed time and help. My plans hadn't developed beyond talking with Bob, Pauly and Burt, which I still had to do. Now it included Norm and that might put my plan, whatever it was going to be, on the fast track. It depended on Norm's willingness to be part of it. And that depended on what he was doing here.

Michael McCloud, Carl Peachey and the Professor were

on stage. McCloud singing his songs of Key West life, backed up by Peachey on the guitar and the Professor on keyboards. The patio crowd loved them.

I walked in from the Lazy Way Lane entrance, scanning the tables as I headed toward the waterside's harbor walk. Coco Joe, a local scoundrel and transplant from L.A., stopped me at the bar and said hi. News of Robin's death hadn't hit the coconut telegraph yet.

Norm sat with the two women and Padre Thomas across from the cigar roller's kiosk, at one of the large, thatched roof tables that filled the dockside end of the patio.

Padre Thomas, the Irish Jesuit who sees and talks to angels. I'm one of the few people in Key West he talks to about the angels. His advice and help have kept me from being killed a number of times and I figured that is good enough reason to listen to him. He often knows things that he shouldn't and the easiest explanation is to believe he gets help from his angels. As I pushed my way through the standing, two-deep crowd around the end of the bar, I wondered if Padre Thomas was here on purpose to see Norm or me.

Norm sat facing me, but his attention went between the women and Padre Thomas, who sat across from them, his back toward me. As if an angel had tapped his shoulder, Padre Thomas turned as I got closer. Dressed in his usual shorts, sandals and buttoned-down collar dress shirt with the sleeves cut off, he held the ever-present cigarette between his fingers. Skinny as a wishbone, thinning hair and piercing blue eyes, Padre Thomas kept his secrets mostly to himself. Without having to look, I knew there'd be two packs of smokes in one of his shirt's pockets and a Budweiser in front of him. He either walks or rides his old conch-cruiser bike around the island.

Norm smiled as if he was glad to see me. So did the two Irish women. Padre Thomas' face held a grim expression. I thought hard to recall the names of the women. They both waved. I forced a smile and clapped Padre Thomas on the back. His expression didn't change.

"Did he drag you both down here?" I pointed to Norm.

"He said he'd flown into Fort Lauderdale and was driving here, so we left Brigid and Seanan with da." She extended her hand. "I'm Nora, we met at McGinty's. This is Peggy, my sister."

I shook Nora's hand. "Yes, I remember."

She had short, chestnut colored hair and wore a T-shirt that promoted the family pub, Naughton's Irish Pub with a large Celtic cross taking up the front of the shirt. All three wore a pub T-shirt in different colors.

Peggy smiled at me but said nothing. Her hair was russet colored, with blonde highlights put in at the salon, and hung straight past her shoulders. You knew they were sisters because of their Irish pug noses and bright indigo eyes.

Alexis walked by and Norm ordered another round of drinks. She knew I drank Kalik. Padre Thomas had his Budweiser. Norm and the women had mixed drinks.

Before the drinks came and any conversation began, Norm stood.

"Let's pick out a cigar, hoss." He draped his arm across my shoulders, excused us from the table, and led me to the kiosk. "What the fuck's goin on?"

We chose two cigars, the seller cut the end and held his lighter flame open for us. We walked past the table to the boardwalk, smoking.

I told Norm more of the truth this time. He listened without interrupting.

"You were in the room?" He had waited for me to finish.

"Yeah, all mirrors and next door the monitors and editing equipment."

"Ten cameras and monitors." Norm almost sounded impressed. "A bit of money. Who the hell would they blackmail in this hell hole?"

"Guys the Russians brought here," I said. "Dixie didn't recognize the men in the videos she saw, so the assumption is they're tourists."

"Begs another question, Mick." Norm turned to face me, his back to the water. "If she told you the truth and it's Russians, then it's gotta be Alexei's group from Miami. We have ears to the ground, why didn't we know about this operation?"

"You can't know everything."

"Yes we can," he said and bit down on his cigar. "Everything."

I didn't want to think about the meaning of that. The NSA debacle scared me enough.

"Why are you here?" I hoped to change the subject.

"I've got the call in," he said, avoiding my question. "It may take a few hours to a day for someone to get back to me on Morgan's whereabouts. It's the weekend, Mick."

"Jesus, Norm," I had to keep myself from shouting. "You track me easily enough, what's taking so long on this? I want the son-of-a-bitch!"

"I'm not a miracle worker, Mick." Norm reached out and held onto my shoulder. "You're in the system. That makes you easy."

"I need something," I said.

"I can only give you what I have, when I have it," he said. "It takes time to be thorough and get it right. You gotta live with it."

"It's more than I have now." I watched Norm look toward the table.

"I hope the priest doesn't scare the girls."

"They're Irish, Norm, priests and nuns have scared the Irish for centuries," I said. "Why are you here?"

"I'm here to help you, now."

"What brought you to Key West?" His avoidance

concerned me.

He pointed to the table. "After I got you out of L.A., I went to McGinty's a few times. Got to talking with Nora. Had dinner before they al! left."

"You tryin' to tell me you flew out to see Nora?" Another surprise. How many more could this day hold for me?

"She's smart, pretty and fun to be with."

He put smart before pretty and I found that curious.

"You like her? I mean as in like, care for?"

"I'm a little too old to call her a girlfriend," he said and smiled as he looked toward Nora. "But, maybe we're building a relationship. And, hoss, her little sister there has eyes for you." He slapped me on the back and we headed to the table as Alexis brought our drinks.

"Norm, I don't have time for this right now."

"What else do you have to do while we're waiting on my phone call?"

"I need to get hold of Bob and Pauly and Burt." I sat next to Padre Thomas.

"I need to talk to you," Padre Thomas whispered barely audible over McCloud's singing.

The grim expression on his face suggested more bad news.

Protected by the Angels
Chapter EIGHT

Norm in a romantic relationship, I thought as I raised my bottle for his toast, I never would have guessed it.

"To the Irish," he said.

We all touched glass.

Padre Thomas went right back to talking with Nora and Peggy in Irish. I drank the beer and said nothing because the expression on his face had changed from grim to . . . well, for Padre Thomas it might have been happy. Norm gave me his 'what-the-hell's-this' stare and I hunched my shoulders.

"Should we get something to eat?" Norm broke into the conversation between the sisters and Padre Thomas.

Music had ended and the entertainers were making one last pitch for McCloud's CDs and Peachey's books.

It occurred to me that I hadn't eaten since breakfast. "I'm hungry."

"The Boathouse still has happy hour prices?" Norm asked about another waterfront restaurant/bar not too far away. "I like its prime rib."

The early grayness of fall fooled me, but it was only five-thirty. "Till seven," I said.

"I have a dinner engagement," Padre Thomas said. "But I need to talk with Mick, so I'll walk along for a minute."

Norm paid Alexis and we took the Harbor Walk toward the Boathouse. The girls pointed to boats in the water and Norm told them his Key West stories. He didn't appear to be a guy who hated the tropics. If I told him I saw changes in him because of Nora, he'd probably punch me.

Padre Thomas slowed and we fell back.

"I'm sorry about Robin," he said in a whisper. "I've prayed for her and her baby and lit a candle."

At this point, I wasn't a big fan of God, so I thanked

Padre Thomas and bit my tongue.

"You should let the police get Morgan," he said in his natural tone of voice. "He deserves to be locked up for the rest of his life."

"I agree, Padre. Every cop in the state is looking for him." How'd he know all this, if the coconut telegraph hadn't kicked in with rumors yet? I didn't ask, because then I'd have to believe in his angels, again.

"And you're planning to look for him, too." He wasn't asking a question.

We passed the old icehouse that's Jimmy Buffett's recording studio. A poorly kept secret location that's known by most, including his fans that flock here at the end of October through the first week of November, following the island's weeklong Fantasy Fest.

Locals filled the Conch Republic Seafood Company's bar and listened to Joel Nelson.

"I want to see Morgan caught," I said. "If I can help I will."

"It's a dangerous pursuit, Mick." He grabbed my arm to stop me. "You'll be putting people's lives in danger. Yours and your friends."

"You're talking in riddles again, Padre."

"I need to go with you." Another surprise to add to the day's long list.

"Go where, Padre?"

"He's with the motorcycle gang," he lowered his voice. "They're bad people, Mick. Dangerous."

"So why do you want to go?" I didn't bother asking how he knew. I'd figured it out.

"To protect you," he said. "The angels will protect us. But Mick, what about the others?"

Like a Dog Chasing its Tail
Chapter NINE

The Boathouse, like Schooner and the Conch Republic Seafood Company, couldn't seat everyone. We stood outside, ordered another drink and waited for Norm's name to be called. Padre Thomas left for wherever and we suddenly became two couples. Norm stayed close to Nora and that left Peggy next to me. The situation made me uncomfortable. Padre Thomas' warning worried me. My thoughts ran in circles, like a dog chasing its tail. I had to play along with Norm while I waited for his phone to ring and, hopefully, provide me with the information I needed on Morgan's whereabouts, so I made the best of it.

"Can you see those two as a couple?" Peggy's pug nose crinkled when she smiled and her eyes sparkled. In spite of her comment, she seemed happy for her sister.

I returned the smile, but doubted my eyes sparkled. "My background with Norm doesn't include his social life."

"Really! What were his words? Oh yeah, you were thick as thieves."

"What else did he say?" Now my curiosity was piqued.

She retold his stories of how he always had to get me out of trouble and used the situation in L.A., at McGinty's, as an example. The stories he told the sisters were partially true. What he failed to add almost made them lies by omission, something we were both good at.

Finally, it was our turn to sit and, after going through the menu, Norm convinced us to have the prime rib. Another round of drinks with dinner and small talk while we ate.

"So, you live here and do nothing?" Nora said as the server cleared away the dishes.

Norm ordered another round but I declined.

"Often doing nothing consumes a lot of time in Key

West," I said. "It's not as easy as it looks."

"I don't understand." Nora looked at Norm so I wasn't sure if she was speaking to me.

"You know, occasionally I'm still a journalist," I said.

Norm gave me one of his looks that said he wondered where I was going with that comment.

"That's how you two met, when Norm saved you from the Colombian cartel," Peggy said.

"I'm sure that's how he remembers it." I wished I'd taken that other beer. "He was tailing me in Panama because I had an interview with a wanted cartel boss who'd come there to hide. Instead of waiting for the interview to be finished, Norm and his guys crashed in. They knew about the bodyguards but came in anyway, with guns firing. I got my ass out of there before the cartel boss figured I'd set him up. Norm's men took me into custody when I got outside. You could say he was the one that got me in trouble . . . and still does."

Both sisters looked at Norm.

"Different points of view," he said. "The important thing is that's how we met. Both of us young and foolish back then. Living in the South Bay area of L.A."

"Today we're older but still fools." I received Norm's evil eyes stare. "Where are you staying?" I wanted to change the subject.

"We have a room at the Mango Tree Inn," Nora said.

I wondered if the *we* included her sister or Norm. "Norm likes that place. Good people own it."

"They like Norm," Nora said. "They had two rooms for him without a problem."

"What are you doing now?" Peggy turned to me. "Are you working on anything?"

"Funny you should ask." It was my turn to toss a hard look at Norm. "It stays among us, right?"

Nora and Peggy nodded, giving me their attention. Norm

frowned and shook his head.

"I'm covering a local murder for a news magazine." I kept my voice low, hoping I sounded conspiratorial. "The cops are being quiet about it, but I got a tip, so they've dealt with me. A little, anyway."

"A murder in Key West?" Nora turned to Norm again.

"It happens," he said.

"Can you tell us about it?" Nora said.

"Not really," I said. "But I'm waiting on a phone call." I looked at Norm. "When it comes I may have to leave. Actually, I should be home waiting for it."

"Can't you help Mick?" Nora poked Norm on the arm. "You have a lot of contacts."

"Yeah, Norm, you could make some calls to the spooks and maybe put me ahead of the cops." I grinned like the Cheshire cat, then put on the best facial grimace I could. "Naw, I can't take him away from you. When the phone call comes, I've gotta head to the mainland."

"But it's a murder case," Peggy whispered. "Don't the police have all the same resources as Norm?"

"I suppose so." I kept looking at Norm, surprised that both women seemed to know something about his background, if not his work. "I really have to excuse myself. I should be home waiting on the call and packing to go. I have a couple of friends that will come with me."

Both sisters turned to Norm.

"Okay," he mumbled, "I can make some calls, but I'm staying, not going on one of his wild goose chases that turn into disasters."

"Norm, you don't have to do that," I said. "I've got dependable friends."

"Yeah, hoss, I've met 'em. They're dependable, if you're looking for trouble."

The sisters seemed excited. I'm not sure why. Maybe because they got some free time of their own.

Opening the Gates to Hell
Chapter TEN

Norm and I compromised. Because of the hour, and it being Saturday, he doubted anyone would get back to him before Sunday, late morning. He'd make more calls in the morning and promised to be at Tita's house – it would always be Tita's house – by 8 A.M. But I wondered if the *in love* Norm would be as punctual as the Norm of old. It felt good knowing the intelligence arm of the country worked on Sunday, I told him as we parted ways at the waterfront.

I left text messages for Bob, Pauly and Burt to come by the house at nine and asked Pauly to bring breakfast and *café con leches* for five from Harpoon Harry's.

The Sunday edition of the local paper had no coverage of Robin's murder. That suggested Richard kept the murder under wraps and hadn't released any incident reports. A few minutes before eight I heard the front door handle rattle. Through the glass panel I could see Norm trying his old door key.

"I got a new door and lock after the fire." I opened the door.

Norm looked around. A few months ago, we had been in the room after the fire department finished cleaning up and almost condemned the house.

"Bob did the remodel?"

"More than he should've," I said. "He put together the crew that did the work and he supervised."

Norm pointed to the master bedroom.

"Guest room." Before Alexei's men killed Tita, we shared that room. Even though I bought new furnishings for it after the remodeling, I still heard her voice and smelled her scent. I kept the door closed.

"Time to let go, Mick." Norm walked to the kitchen.

"I'm living here, aren't I?" Two years ago, I thought I'd never be back, so living here showed I'd almost let go.

He looked at the cold espresso machine.

"Coffee and breakfast are on the way." We sat down. "What've you heard?"

"I made the call before you showed up yesterday," he said. "Still waiting on the return call."

"I know you did. I didn't know what Nora knew or didn't know about you."

"I haven't lied, if that's what you mean. She knows there are things I can't discuss."

"I picked up on her not knowing the whole truth." I smirked. "Makes it tough on a relationship."

"When and if this becomes a relationship," he lied, "I'll let you know."

"Do that," I said. There was something else I needed to bring to his attention, but I had no clue as to how he'd react.

"What are you worried about, hoss?" Norm guessed something was wrong from my demeanor.

"I don't need you getting pissed at me." Without thinking, I pushed my chair away from the table, distancing us, out of his striking range.

He said nothing but his stare spoke volumes.

"She knows who you are," I said quietly. "Seámus knew we were together and that you pulled me out of the SAS interrogation. Back in the day, he financed their da's pub. If her family knows Seámus, they knew Cecil."

"Make your point, Mick." Norm opened and closed his fists, finally interlocking the fingers and cracking his knuckles.

"In Skerries, I learned not to underestimate Irishwomen, Norm. That's all I'm saying." I met his eyes as I spoke. "You've gotta take into consideration that her family is old IRA. They know you're close to the SAS."

"So, what's she doing? She lookin' for inside info on the

Brits?" He sent me an unfriendly smirk. "She couldn't like me for me?"

"Hell, Norm, half the time I don't like you because you're you and we're friends." I hoped we were, I thought as the words came out. "Think with the head on your shoulders, not other body parts."

"Yes Mum," he said and winked. "Where's my breakfast?"

I didn't buy it. He walked away unconcerned about my comments and without protest.

"You had her checked out!" I said. "Son of a bitch!"

"You think? We're friends, but I had you thoroughly checked out after Panama," he said. "I like Nora. She's smart and pretty and her da has no connection to the current IRA or Gerry Adams."

"That's a start." I wondered about it and knew Adams and the IRA had fooled the British, why not an American query. The IRA always kept its secrets. Could da be one of them?

Bob walked in before I could say anything more. Maybe for the best.

Upon seeing Norm, Bob grabbed him and gave him a Texas bear hug. Burt showed up as the hug ended and seemed glad to see Norm too.

Pauly came with the five breakfasts and *café con leches* while the small talk went on. Only Pauly gave me a quizzical look as he greeted Norm.

We sat in the kitchen, ate our breakfasts and drank the coffee as they all kidded Norm about Nora. He hadn't told them much, but they assumed he came with a woman. Fortunately for me, Peggy's name didn't come up.

Pauly broke the revelry. "Why'd you call us?" He looked at Norm.

They followed me to the back porch. I told them about Robin, the blackmail, possible connection to Alexei, and that I needed their help to go after Morgan.

"Norm's using his resources to try and locate Morgan," I said, finally.

"How's that going?" Pauly's skepticism came with the question.

"Waiting," Norm said. "It's only been twenty-four hours and, for all Mick knows, this Morgan is gone to ground here in Key West."

"What are the cops doing?" Bob said.

"Richard promised to call as soon as they had him," I said. "The FDLE has the BOLO with his photo and description and so does the Marine Patrol."

"Hurry up and wait?" Burt rolled one end of his bushy mustache. "Had that in the Navy."

"If he went to the Russians for help, they'd get him out here," Pauly said. "Maybe dump his body from a plane into the Atlantic."

"If he's that stupid," I said. "He grabbed the money and the DVDs, so maybe he's bringing them to the Rattlers."

"Motorcycle gang." Burt shook his head.

"Motorcycle gang with meth and strip club connections," Norm said. "Not the type of guys you want your sister to bring home."

"Obviously," I said thinking of Robin. "When he's located, I'm going after him."

"And do what?" Norm said.

"When the time comes, I'll figure it out."

No one spoke for a few minutes.

"Five of us against the Rattlers?" Bob said. "They ain't good odds, Mick."

"Five of us to grab Morgan," I said. "I don't wanna go up against the Rattlers. We find him alone, or with only a few. We get him."

"Guys," Norm cut me off. "As I told Mick last night, my help stops with locating this guy, if I can. It's the four of you."

"We need Texas Rich," Bob said. "Why not let the FDLE get Morgan?"

"I want him first," I said.

The four of them turned to me waiting for more. I wanted to kill Morgan, but didn't say it aloud.

"He can give me a name, maybe a location of the Russians he dealt with," I said instead. "It might get me closer to Alexei."

Again, silence followed my comment.

Pauly kept eyeing Norm. They had a thing, Pauly being an ex-smuggler and Norm a government man. They've come together to help me before.

"Mick, Norm or no Norm, I'd go to the gates of hell with you," Pauly said. "I want you to know that. But, I stop at the gate, Mick. So plan this out as best you can. Know what you can expect from me, but know my limits too."

To Help or Not
Chapter ELEVEN

I didn't wanna go as far as the gates of hell, as Pauly called it. What I wanted to do was get the son-of-a-bitch Morgan . . . Killing him would've been my first gut reaction, but that wouldn't bring Robin back or get me closer to Alexei. I'd settle for knowing he wasted away in a prison where he faced daily bullying by men a lot more sadistic than him.

"I understand, Pauly," I said. "I'm not asking anyone here to commit to that situation, including me. I wanna snatch him and bring him to Key West. Find out about his Russian contacts. They could get me closer to Alexei. I have no desire to take on the Rattlers."

No one replied. Not even Norm. I looked around the room and had been in life-threatening situations with everyone there; most recently in the backyard of the house as Cuban gunmen tried to kill us because they thought I knew of their forged art scheme. It happened without any pre-warning and somehow we all fell into place and defended those innocents who had come for Texas Rich's barbecue. Our choices were few but, now with time to think about outcomes, everyone thought too hard.

"Bob, aren't the SEALS noted for snatching terrorists from their hideouts?" I turned to Bob, knowing about his SEAL background.

Bob laughed. "Oh yeah, with years of training, practice and intel."

"Mick, I don't think anyone is saying no to you," Pauly said. "Well, maybe Norm is, in a way. We're only saying we gotta take it slow. I dealt with the Rattlers in my other life," he looked toward Norm who didn't believe in ex-drug smugglers. "Together they're bad asses, with a ruthless mob mentality. You can't deal with them. Your only choice is to kill them!"

"We'll make our own intel," I said. "When we know where he is, we watch, we do surveillance, we listen and when the opportunity offers itself, we snatch him. I'm not talking about walking into one of their hangouts, guns blazing, and taking Morgan."

"And if that's the only way?" Norm said.

I said what they needed to hear. "We call Richard and he sends in the FDLE." I wondered if anyone believed me.

I never got to find out because Norm's cell phone rang. He answered it and walked down the porch steps into the yard. Norm ended the phone call and put his cell away as he walked back.

"I need your laptop and printer," he said.

They were on a small table I used as a desk in the living room. Norm sat down, turned the laptop on, went to the Internet, and signed into his email account. He began printing a document from an email.

"There's not much," he said as the printer stopped. "But they found him and he's out of the Keys. They have eyes on him, now."

Norm took the five printed pages, scanned them and then handed them to me.

"Morgan got to Daytona Beach," Norm continued. "He's with two men believed to be members of the Rattlers out of the Panhandle. Cameras picked him up on I-95."

"You said Daytona, that's on the East Coast of the state," Burt said.

"They left Daytona this morning heading east toward Ocala," Norm said. "Assumption is the Panhandle."

"Where they've got their meth labs. Last page." I shook the page. "They make and distribute meth and have interests in strip clubs in Florida, Alabama and Louisiana."

"Nothing on the Russians being involved with the Rattlers," Norm said. "So the deal Morgan had going in Key

West had nothing to do with the Rattlers."

Padre Thomas stood in the doorway leading to the kitchen. No one had heard him enter.

"You can't go without me," he said and we all looked toward him.

"Padre, we haven't made plans to go anywhere," I said. "We're only wondering if we should."

"Of course," he said. "But in case you change your mind, I'll spend the afternoon here."

He leaned on the porch railing, not far from Norm.

"Do you know where on I-95?" I said.

Norm shook his head. "Facial recognition on a highway cam. Once they had him, it was all over."

"So, FDLE could have him too?" I said.

"Possible, if they have the right equipment," Norm said.

"It's the weekend, Mick," Padre Thomas said. "FDLE is not running on full office staff."

I wondered why he spoke. He wouldn't mention the angels in front of everyone. Bob tolerated Padre Thomas for me, but deep down his Texas upbringing made a Catholic priest questionable. Burt believed in everything and nothing, depending on the situation and Norm was kind of that way too.

Norm stared at Padre Thomas, finally grinned and nodded. "Yeah, more than likely, but my team has eyes on Morgan and will text me updates and call if it looks like he's headed anywhere but the Panhandle."

"In Ocala they can connect to roads in all directions," Pauly said. "Not just west to the Panhandle."

"They are not going to the Panhandle. They have meth labs off state route 40," Padre Thomas said.

"Where on 40?" Norm said.

"They have a good location for the lab," Padre said. "It will not be in a trailer."

Padre Thomas' comments met with silence. I'm not sure,

but there didn't seem to be the enthusiastic support that I had encountered in the past from these men.

"We have to wait for confirmation, Padre," I said to break the silence. I would've gone with Padre Thomas' information, but I had the beginnings of doubt about the others.

"You should plan anyway." Norm's suggestion surprised me. "Are you limiting yourself to the Panhandle?"

"No," I said before considering I only spoke for myself. "I want to know where he's gone."

"We'll need vehicles," Bob said.

"I've got my Jeep," Pauly said. "Mick's got the old white Jeep. That's two."

"Yours has doors," Bob said. "Mick's is open and it may be cool up there."

"My truck can sit four," Burt said. "A small back seat."

"What's your idea?" I looked at Bob.

"I don't have a plan, that's your job," Bob said. "But I know what's needed for gathering intel and for the grab. We don't want any one vehicle to stand out. My guess is these guys are already paranoid so we don't want to feed that."

"I can pull together the weapons," Pauly said.

We all focused on Pauly. His comment brought us back to reality.

"Better to have them unused than wished we brought 'em," he said.

Mick Murphy's Law
Chapter TWELVE

Support came out of nowhere and it seemed all were onboard with helping me get Morgan. What happened? What had I missed? No one squealed when Pauly mentioned weapons and we all knew what kind of firepower he had available. No one ever asked how or where he got the weapons. We knew better. A half-hour ago, I thought I'd lost any chance of their help.

"Any of you geniuses have a map of Florida?" Norm sat on the new couch.

"Norm, get with it." Bob went to the computer. "You want a map of Florida, you Google."

"Google's replaced the neighborhood gas station, too?" Norm got up and stood behind Bob. "The northern part of the state. We need road maps. Include the Panhandle."

Padre Thomas tapped Norm on the shoulder. "You should have maps of route 40, too. It goes through a national forest."

"Maps from Daytona to Ocala, too," Norm said.

I wondered how he knew route 40 went through Ocala, but Norm is always full of surprises. A little voice kept whispering in my ear, *Need to find out how Norm knew that.*

Bob printed out the maps.

"A gas station map would've unfolded. We all could've seen the damn thing." Norm looked at the small maps as he walked to thc kitchen.

We gathered around the table and watched him find the map of route 40 and move his finger across from Daytona Beach to Ocala. With a side look at Padre Thomas, he went to another map and kept his finger moving along I-75 to I-10 to state route 231 and south to Panama City.

"Ocala is less than a two-hour ride from Daytona and we

know this Morgan is on 40. It goes through the Ocala National Forest and some small towns." He returned to route 40. "It wouldn't be the first time some bad guys used state or federal forests for drug production. Lot of space and little security. Hard to keep track of all the open space."

"You think it's possible they set up meth labs in the forest?" I looked at how big the area was and doubted the authorities patrolled it thoroughly. "There are small towns around the forest."

"Small and easy to avoid. The Rattlers have kept the move a secret, if they're there, and it's hard to keep secrets from us," Norm said, meaning JSOC, not us. "Maybe they're expanding to the East Coast. If they're using a trailer as a lab, they can put it anywhere in there."

"It's not a trailer," Padre Thomas said but no listened.

"Daytona has its share of strip clubs," Bob said. "If the Rattlers are into them too, it might be logical. Motorcycle bars, strip clubs, tourists, college kids."

"A smorgasbord of customers," Pauly said.

"Of victims," Padre Thomas said.

Norm's phone rang. He answered and walked to the back porch. He returned shortly and didn't look happy.

"Well, Padre, you might be right." He stared at Padre Thomas. "Morgan should have passed Ocala onto I-75 by now and he hasn't. Satellite lost him in the national forest."

"What's next?" I said.

"People are doing me a favor, Mick." Norm paced the small kitchen. He looked into the fridge. "Next is, we wait to see if he gets picked up by a highway camera on I-75. I only had the satellite for a short time."

"What other routes could he have taken?" I said.

Norm leaned over one of the small maps, moved the sheets of paper around until he found the one he wanted. He pointed at the dim gray line on the black-and-white map.

"Could've taken route seventeen toward Lake George or

south to DeLand," he said. "Anyone familiar with those places?"

"Google." Bob went back to the computer in the living room. We followed. "Lake George doesn't offer much as population goes, campgrounds and boating. DeLand is small, compared to what's on the other side of I-95, and has a general aviation airport."

Norm gave a side look toward Padre Thomas. "Meth labs in the forest and small aircraft for delivery. Sounds like the Rattlers are expanding their market share."

"What do they need Morgan for?" I said. "What's he bringing them? If he didn't mention he's wanted, they'll kill him if he draws attention to their operation."

"Is this something you could exchange for more favors?" Bob looked up from the computer toward Norm. "Do you want to pass it on to Richard?"

"Richard can't help us. Morgan's out of the jurisdiction of the local cops." Norm turned to face me. "My experience with local and state cops is just like the FBI and CIA, they don't communicate."

"So we're on our own?" Burt said.

"If you want to tell Richard what you have, he'd want to know how you got it. A cop's nature." Norm looked at each of us before he continued. "Everything I've done is off the books. I'd look Richard in the eyes and deny everything. That's one problem in telling Richard."

"There's another?" Burt seemed to be looking for an answer that made sense to him.

"Yeah, Burt, Richard's a cop and he'd feel obligated to pass on whatever you told him and that leads back to my denying everything. It goes up a notch when the state cops are involved."

"Okay," I said. "What options are we left with?"

"Your usual bullshit, Mick," Norm said. "We go find Morgan. When located, we tell the cops." Norm grinned. "Of course Murphy's Law kicks in and it'll all go to hell before that."

The Angels Are On Our Side
Chapter THIRTEEN

"He's at least eight hours ahead of us." Pauly looked at the map Norm had his hand on. "I could fly us up there. Rent a car or two. Take away that advantage."

"Except we'd be trading in recon ability for speed." Norm turned and faced us. "We need three vehicles." He turned back to the maps. "Two up I-75, in case he goes that way to the Panhandle. The other up I-95 to Daytona and pick up 40, where he was last spotted."

"If Morgan's gone to ground and we have no information on him, then what?" I said.

"At some point all our vehicles will be on 40." Norm made a circle of the large areas with his finger. "We're looking for bikers, an old trailer being towed, and hope he's somewhere between us."

"It's not a trailer," Padre Thomas said but again, no one listened.

"We need a meeting up spot," Bob said. "There's a marina with a restaurant on 40. Astor Bridge Marina. People come and go."

"What do you know about the area?" Norm said.

"Never been there," Bob said, "but I know people that have camped along the St. Johns River and Lake George. "

"Campgrounds mean people," Norm said.

"Maybe it's not season, this time of year," Burt said. "Cool up there. Cold at night."

"Okay. Let's back up. We still have to get there. Three vehicles. Pauly's Jeep, Burt's truck. What else do we have?"

"My pick up has a back seat," Bob said. "If we need it."

"Like Burt said, probably too cold up there, so forget your open Jeep." Norm looked at me. "I'll get one from JIATF on the base."

Norm had called on his contacts at the Joint Inter-Agency Task Force at the Navy base before. All bad memories, but on the positive side, we survived. Last time I was in a JIATF vehicle, Tita got shot and I had to kill a drug cartel assassin by the Key West Cemetery. Yeah, bad memories.

"We should add Texas Rich," Bob said. "He can be counted on in a tight situation. He's proven that."

Recently, Texas Rich had put on a barbecue at Tita's and it came to an end minutes before the Cuban art forgers attacked. His quick thinking got the few party stragglers to safety.

"One more can't hurt," Norm said. "We need a van or SUV with tinted windows for transporting this guy."

"That's the cops' problem," I said. We all knew I lied.

Pauly looked at his wristwatch. "It's three. How do we want to do this?"

My lie lived and no one mentioned it.

"We've got one other thing to consider," Norm said. "What's Morgan got that the Rattlers want? Maybe a blackmail scheme and how to use the strip clubs for it? But, if he's putting their meth operation in jeopardy, he could be dead and buried by now and that's why the satellite lost him."

No one spoke. Eyes turned to me. After all, I wanted Morgan and my friends were offering to help. This was my doing and they looked to me for answers. I didn't know what to say.

"He's not dead." We all turned to Padre Thomas.

"Gut feeling, Padre?" Norm said.

Padre Thomas shook his head. "The forest and Daytona. He's part of the gang now."

Norm grinned. "I want to err on the side of caution, Padre, so you'll forgive me if we stick to my plan. You can't tell us where in the forest he is, can you?"

"Not near the camp grounds," he said. "He's in the forest,

off the river."

"The meth lab?" Norm seemed interested.

Padre Thomas nodded. "Yes. And motorcycles."

"It wouldn't be a motorcycle gang without 'em," Norm said. "Okay. It's three, we meet back here in two hours. Pauly, that enough time?"

"Yeah, plenty," he said. "We going to leave in the dark?"

"Depends," Norm said. "I should have another call by six and that may tell us what's changed or not, we'll decide then."

"I'll get Texas Rich and be back," Bob said. "I'm going to the boat and pack some things. We might be gone for a few days."

* * *

As the guys left I remembered Nora and Peggy and the things Norm had said last night. And again this morning, Norm made a point of saying he wouldn't be going with us because he wanted to stay with Nora. What had happened?

Norm's arrival usually sets off my paranoia. He couldn't have known ahead of time about Robin's murder and Morgan's running back to the Rattlers when he made plans to come to Key West. I kept repeating that to myself.

"Norm," I said as he straightened up the small maps. "We're no longer concerned about Nora and her sister?"

The smile became an impish grin. "You owe me for this one, hoss."

"I don't buy it Norm."

"What am I selling?"

"A few hours ago, Nora was your priority," I said. "Now you're helping plan this and leaving Nora behind. Why?"

Norm took a beer out of the fridge, offered me one. I accepted it as he sat at the table. "Mick, you and your buddies could run circles around me in Key West." He took a long pull on the beer. "Hell, maybe even to Marathon. Eight hours up the road, you're like babes in the woods."

"We need you! Is that what you're saying?"

"Somethin' along those lines." He took another swallow of beer. "I gave Nora a lot of thought. She's not going anywhere. She and Peggy have been down here on their own before. They know a few bartenders and restaurant staff. They'll get along without me."

"And I can't?" My beer was gone.

"Nora and her sister want me to help you." The impish grin again. "Both of them will understand and probably thank me."

"For taking care of me!"

"Semantics," he said. "Taking care of you or helping you. It all comes down to our being together."

Norm dropped his beer bottle in the recycle bin and stood in the kitchen door looking at the backyard with his back to me.

"What Padre Thomas said concerns me." No wonder he kept his back to me. I'm not sure Norm could've said that to me with a straight face. He always questions Padre Thomas, even to the point of calling him an impostor at one time. Now he had concerns because of the *impostor's* insight.

"Make sense, Norm! Why are you suddenly paying attention to what he says?" I waited to hear his reply.

"The people I'm dealing with on the phone." Norm hesitated. "No one hides from them."

"You mean Morgan or the Rattlers?"

"I mean *no one!*" His eyes looked as cold as I'd ever seen them. "The Rattlers and other outlaw bikers are on the agency's watch list, hoss. Clubhouses bugged, phones monitored, emails read, members followed. The agency had no chatter on Morgan's Key West scheme or that the Rattlers were east of I-75. They're concerned to the point of worry. That concerns me and then the good padre mentions Morgan's in the forest. Maybe you didn't notice but he had authority in his voice and it sent chills up my spine. Just those few words and I, ah, believed him. I've dealt with Central American shamans before, but I never doubted what they did had to be a trick. Padre Thomas' knowledge is puzzling. Like the druids before him, knowledge is power."

"You're afraid of Padre Thomas's knowledge or how he gets it?" Norm surprised me with his honesty. At least, I wanted to believe he spoke honestly.

"No, hoss, I ain't afraid of Padre Thomas. If what he says is true we're in a shit pot of trouble." Norm walked to the porch.

I stood at the railing looking toward the gazebo.

"He said he could protect me," I said. "That's why he wants to come. He also said he couldn't protect the others. Actually, he said the angels would protect him and me."

"Let him come." Norm's voice came steady, not joking about the angels. "It can't hurt to have the angels on our side."

9mm Sig Sauer P250
Chapter FOURTEEN

"I'm calling Jim Ashe, to arrange for the Jeep." Norm walked to the front porch and paced as he talked on the phone. Jim Ashe, a captain at JIATF, someone who had worked with Norm in Key West before.

"Should have asked you if you needed anything from Ashe." Norm closed the door.

"Like what?"

"A bazooka?" He smiled. "A tommy-gun?"

"I have my Sig," I said. "Now I need to load extra magazines."

My semi-automatic 9mm Sig Sauer P250 had been my gun of choice for a long time. I knew my limitations with it and knew what it and I could and couldn't do.

"Pauly brings the toys. Someone from the base will drop the Jeep." Norm walked around the room, checking the walls and windows. "A lot different than last time I was here."

"Yeah." I went to the bedroom and brought my gun bag out. I removed eight 9mm magazines and four boxes of hollow-point bullets.

Norm laughed to himself as I began loading the magazines on the coffee table.

"Something funny?"

"I was just thinking," he said. "Eight magazines. No matter how many you have, you only got two choices."

"And what are they?"

"You're bringing too many," he said and then shook his head. "Or not enough."

His simple words held a lot of truth if you considered our past experiences together.

"You really plan to give this guy to the cops?" Norm changed the subject as he watched me.

"I think so." I don't know if I lied or not.

"Doesn't sound like you."

"What sounds like me, killing him?"

"Yeah. Once you get whatever info he has on Alexei or Alexei's men, that sounds like you."

"I want to kill Alexei, Norm. Up close and personal. I want him to know it's me putting a bullet between his eyes." I stopped loading the magazines. "It's about Tita, it's about me, it's about sinking the *Fenian Bastard*. It's personal."

"And beating to death a pregnant woman you knew isn't personal?"

I nodded. "Okay, it is personal. But different."

"How's it different?"

"Jesus Norm, you sound like you want me to kill him."

"I think killing him and however many bikers we have to is gonna be easier than taking him alive."

"If it comes to that, I don't have a problem."

"But you wanna try and take him and give him to the cops."

"Norm, I want the fucker to suffer." I looked up, wishing him to understand. "I want him to spend the rest of his life in prison, finding out what being bullied feels like. I'm hoping some con named Bubba makes him his bitch and he lives to be a hundred."

"There's that too," he said. "We got the two options and we take the first one that comes."

"Fine with me." I took the cloth out of my gun bag, spread it over the coffee table and began to take my Sig apart to clean.

"I'm off to see Nora," Norm said, looking about as sly as a guy that uses dynamite to fish. "The Jeep's here." He looked out the window. "You okay?"

"Sure, why wouldn't I be?"

"Just asking." He closed the door as he left.

Texas Rich called and said he and Bob were picking up

sandwiches at El Siboney. Six Cuban mix and six ham and cheese. Leftovers for the ride north, he said.

At four-thirty, I realized I hadn't called Richard since talking to him yesterday. Knowing me as he does, he had to think that strange. I called him.

"I thought you'd drowned," he said as a greeting without humor.

"Spending some time with friends visiting." It wasn't a total lie.

"Yes, I heard Norm was here." Another person telling me I couldn't keep secrets from him.

I hesitated for a moment. "Yeah, he came down with two Irish girls we know from Fort Lauderdale."

"Why do I have a hard time picturing Norm and any woman together?" He sounded like he wanted to laugh.

"Before you break into hysterics." My tone turned cold without my planning it. "Any word on Morgan?"

"No, Mick, nothing." Richard returned to his business tone of voice. "FDLE is looking for him outside the county, sheriff's looking in the Keys and we're checking in case he's gone to ground in Key West. That enough for you?"

"No sightings? Nothing?"

"Like smoke in the wind," he said. "We found an address book at the house that appears to be his, so locally we've checked each address. We've shared county and statewide addresses with the authorities. Even out of state law enforcement. And Mick, there's not a cop alive that doesn't want to take down someone who killed a woman and her unborn child."

"I know, Richard." My tone softened. "I'm frustrated."

"How do you think we feel?" He paused. "What are you doing now?"

"I took a break and left Norm with the Irish girls."

"Not planning anything stupid, are you?"

"With the girls?"

MICK MURPHY'S LAW/*Michael Haskins*

"Don't be an asshole."

"Maybe Norm and I are going to Fort Lauderdale with them," I lied. "You'll call me as soon as you know anything, right?"

"Before I call my command staff, I'll call you, promise."

"Thank you, Richard, I appreciate it." I wondered if he believed me, as I hung up.

Military Tactics and How to Kill
Chapter FIFTEEN

Bob and Texas Rich showed up first, with sandwiches and beer, followed soon after by Padre Thomas. He might have been a skinny, frail, homeless-looking man, but his determination reminded me of a pit bull with its jaws clamped onto your leg. Padre Thomas' faith that the angels would protect us both led him to decide hastily to tag along, and that worried me because I didn't share his blind beliefs.

Burt and Pauly arrived at the same time. Norm showed up at five-thirty. The small talk of anxious men stopped when he walked in, and the kidding began. It came out friendly and hid our surprise at seeing the gentler side of Norm. When he looked close to being pissed off, I cut in.

"Okay, we can discuss Norm's love life later." I stood. "Let's put some order to what we're doing and a time frame. Norm, have you received the update?"

Norm looked at his wristwatch. "I expect to in fifteen minutes."

"Pauly, you walked in empty-handed." As I spoke, everyone turned to him. The availability of weapons he had access to surprised us more often than not.

"While Norm was out diddling his girlfriend, I put together three packages. One for each vehicle. They're in the Jeep and I wasn't going to drag them in here, just to take back out as we leave." Pauly grinned.

Norm frowned. I figured he wanted to pounce on Pauly, so I shook my head and he stayed sitting. Their agreement to disagree sometimes took them to the verbal ropes. I hoped that it didn't go further.

"Two cars up I-75 to Ocala and route 40," I said. "Pauly, Bob in one, Texas Rich and Burt in the second car. Norm and I go up I-95 to Daytona."

"Who do I go with?" Padre Thomas needed to be included.

"Me," I said.

"Why the split?" Burt believed in team playing and splitting up concerned him.

"The last spot Morgan was seen is the Ocala National Forest, on 40," I said. "We know the Rattlers have at least one strip club in Daytona to the east and its headquarters somewhere in the Panhandle, near Panama City, to the west. Forty takes them from Daytona to I-75, which leads to the Panhandle."

"Why don't we go to the Panhandle?" Bob, too, showed concern for splitting up our small team.

"There's a possibility Morgan and his Rattlers friends are staying in the National Forest." I looked at Padre Thomas, since that's what he said the angels told him. "When you guys reach 40, go east. See what's to see. Biker bars, strip clubs, trailer courts they could set up a meth lab in."

"Also, watch for a . . . what do you call a gang of bikers? A pod, a gaggle?" Norm got a laugh as the guys threw out their own colorfully vulgar suggested names. Padre Thomas' ears must have been burning. It seemed that Norm had let Pauly's remark pass.

"Whatever they're called, watch for them on the road." Norm continued. "If they pass you, we go to the Panhandle."

"They pass us?" Pauly said. "Then what?"

"No quick U-turns," Norm said. "You and Bob keep a mile or so apart. If you see them, call Bob so he can turn around before they pass and follow them. Then you call us and we all follow Bob."

"What do we know about them and their firepower?" Bob said.

"They're outlaw bikers, bad asses," I said. "They run the meth along the Gulf States and, it seems, they want to branch out to Northern Florida and the East Coast. Figure they're armed while riding and maybe even an Uzi in a saddle bag."

"Forget your Marlon Brando biker images," Norm said, his tone serious. "After Vietnam, vets joined the gang, took over and used their military training to turn it into a profitable and dangerous drug distribution business. They know military tactics and how to kill."

"That's a long time ago," Burt said.

"Yeah, and most of the Nam vets are dead or in jail," Norm said. "But the gang recruited from Gulf War vets, Iraq and Afghanistan vets too, and many of them are delusional and dangerous. Think of the Rattlers as a bad-ass battalion of Army Rangers."

"You gotta be shitting me!" Bob said.

"No, I'm not," Norm said. "They're organized and some of their foot soldiers are dirt-bag bikers like in the *Wild One*. They're the expendables. They do the grunt work. Decision makers and individual club leaders are all ex-military. They're disciplined. Demand it from their members. They follow orders, know how to fight and to kill. We don't want to take them on."

"No we don't," I said. "We want to find Morgan and separate him from the bikers. Bob, that's where your SEAL training comes in."

Bob laughed. "Training is the operative word there, Mick. We knew our target because we did surveillance, had good intel." He shook his head. "Hell, you've got nothing to work with. Sorry."

"Okay, so this is more a seat-of-our-pants operation," Norm said to fill the gap of silence I'd left. "Bob's right. We need surveillance and that's our first priority, once we've located Morgan. No cowboy shit and goin' in to get him at first sighting. Right?"

Everyone nodded, even Padre Thomas.

"Okay then," Norm said. "Let's eat and wait for my call." He checked his wristwatch.

On the Road Again
Chapter SIXTEEN

Norm's cell rang as he finished his beer, a few minutes past six. He answered and walked to the back porch.

We'd eaten the sandwiches and washed them down with a beer. No one wanted to be drunk in case we headed out tonight or leave tomorrow with a hangover. One with the sandwich and that was all.

"No sighting," Norm said as he came back into the kitchen. "We leave at five tomorrow morning. Eight hours to Daytona?" He looked at me and I nodded.

"More than eight hours to Ocala and then another two across to Daytona," Pauly said.

"We'll check the strip club out, get the rooms and then meet you in . . ." Norm waited on Bob.

"Astor," Bob said.

"Everyone knows where they're going and what to do, right?"

Yeses came from everyone.

"Be careful with Pauly's package, it could blow."

"Norm!" Pauly said, faking surprise. "It's all government issue. Have faith my man."

"Government issue?" Norm laughed. "Hell, then it probably won't work."

An operation of any kind, big or small, causes angst and sometimes the best way to deal with it is with humor, or as close to it as you can get. Angst brings caution and caution saves lives, usually, because there's only one guarantee and that is it's gonna get tricky.

"Gas up tonight," I said. "Give me the receipts and I'll pay you back when this is over."

"I'm going to the inn," Norm said. "I'll be here at four, you be awake?"

"I'm not sure I can sleep."

"You're no good to anyone tired," he said. "Get some sleep."

Norm and the others left. Padre Thomas sat on the couch.

"Will you be here on time?"

"I'm here now." Padre Thomas patted the couch. He wasn't going anywhere.

* * *

Norm woke Padre Thomas at four-forty-five, not four like he said. I heard him knocking on the door. I'd slept, but not well. I took a quick shower and when I came out a *café con leche* from Sandy's sat on the table for me. I thanked Norm, but I doubted it took forty-five minutes to get the coffee. We loaded the four-door government Jeep with my duffel bag of clothing and gun case. I didn't mention anything to Norm about being late.

"I think Pauly figures on blowing up the meth lab." Norm opened Pauly's duffel bag of weapons and removed a 12-gauge pump shotgun. "Look what comes with this." He took out a bandolier with 50 shells. "All of them are Dragon Breath shells. Remind you of the good ole days, hoss?"

Almost twenty years ago, Norm had saved me from a revenge-craved Filipino and in the process I destroyed my condo, and a few others below and above mine, when I fired at him with a shotgun using Dragon Breath shells. The shells contain pellets and shards of magnesium and burn whatever they hit.

"Let's not go there," I said as Padre Thomas walked out of the house. "I don't need those memories haunting me right now."

Norm put the shotgun and bandolier away, sealed the duffel bag and laid it on the back floor.

"I'll drive." Norm got in the driver's seat, Padre Thomas in back and I had shotgun.

I wondered if Padre Thomas would consider that an omen?

We left late, closer to five-thirty than five and Norm never mentioned why he ran late.

"You drive from Florida City," Norm said.

"Okay." I watched the sleepy morning streets of Key West as the free-range cocks crowed the arrival of daylight. "We need to follow the turnpike to Fort Pierce and then cut over to I-95. Rush hour traffic to Fort Lauderdale and that area will be bad on ninety-five at this hour."

"How long do you think?" Norm drove out of Key West. "Still eight hours?"

"Gas and food stops, maybe eight hours," I said. "Give or take."

"Padre, we gonna be okay?" Norm looked at Padre Thomas in the rearview mirror.

"I'll pray for a safe trip." He leaned back, the black beads already in his hands as his fingers worked on the first decade of the rosary.

* * *

The ride took too long because most of it was monotonous. We stopped at the Fort Pierce exit and ate breakfast sandwich meals. Norm remembered the extra sandwiches Texas Rich brought last night. We'd all forgotten them. We ate like hyenas while Padre Thomas picked at his food. Thank the fast-food gods when you're driving long distances. Norm drove after we ate.

Padre Thomas' angels watched over us because, even in the construction zones of I-95, we kept moving at fifty-five, while in the normal flow of traffic we sped along at seventy.

Nora and her sister Peggy had Googled motels/hotels in Daytona and found one that Norm liked. Not a chain and not on the water. In Daytona not Daytona Beach. When we'd used a rest stop on the interstate, Norm put the address of the hotel into the GPS.

"The Hideaway? You've got to be kidding," I said when I saw the name of the hotel.

"Laugh," he said, "but it has seven rooms available. It's off any main street and far enough away from the tourist traps to keep strangers from wandering the street."

"It's off International Raceway," I said. "That's where the Daytona Race Track is!"

"It's more than four miles from the track," he said.

At 1 PM we pulled up to the two-story, L-shaped motel. Parking in front and back. Norm registered all seven rooms.

"No calls," I said as I unlocked my room. "Is that good news or bad?"

"Bad news travels fast." Norm went into his room.

"You going in Padre?"

"I thought we'd share a room." Padre Thomas opened the door and looked inside, as if expecting the devil himself. I shook my head and he left for this room.

I'd learned long ago, while covering the drug wars in Mexico and Central America, not to unpack. The one time I did, I had minutes to avoid a pick-up truck of cartel henchmen and ended up leaving everything behind.

My toiletries went into the large bathroom, but my other things stayed in the duffel bag. The room had two double beds and all the goodies that come with hotel rooms these days. Everything worked. I would've been impressed but knew I wouldn't be spending much time in the room.

I opened my laptop and through Google found a map of Astor, Florida. I copied down the address of one marina, so Norm could put it into the GPS. I noticed campgrounds along the Saint Johns River and state road 17 heading north and south not too far away. Route 40 ran right through the center of the Lake George State Forest that bordered on the Ocala National Forest. Lot of wilderness to get lost in and not more than an hour or so from Daytona.

"I got a real map from the office." Norm walked in. He spread the map out on the bed. "Lot of forest, lot of lakes."

"Think he's hidden out there?" I stared at the map with its green forests and blue rivers and lakes.

"Yeah, but they ain't mountain men, hoss. They need to move the meth, so there's a road nearby," Norm said.

"There are no mountains, anyway." It was useless chatter to hear myself talk. It kept me from admitting how nervous this whole thing had made me. When the nervousness sprouted, I remembered Robin and the promise I'd made. I planned to keep it.

I called Pauly while Norm studied the map. They were eating at a roadside marina, off route 40 in Silver Springs.

"The few bikes we saw the guys wore helmets," Pauly said between bites of whatever he had for lunch. "They weren't Rattlers. Lot of trees, man, and fire roads. Would he use a fire road?'

We agreed to meet at the Astor Marina at three.

Padre Thomas came into the room and sat on the one chair. "I heard you say we meet up at three," he said. "What do we do for a couple of hours?"

"We cruise by the Tit-4-Tat strip club, Padre," Norm said.

A Quick Recon
Chapter SEVENTEEN

The Tit-4-Tat strip club didn't use flashy neon signs to shout out for customers, nor life-sized cutouts of scantily clad women or list drink special prices. No billboard-sized greetings welcoming passersby, coaxing them in, flickered down from the rooftop. A small sign with the club's name, attached above the front door to the nondescript, square, two-story building, became visible only if you knew where to look. A street light, two buildings away, offered the only evening illumination to the front lot.

The half-dozen parking spots out front probably never filled up. A narrow driveway led to the back and there a large lot waited for Harleys. A doublewide door to the back entrance remained locked at two o'clock in the afternoon. Small strip mall businesses backed up to the rear lot and a short row of stores fanned out on both sides of the building. The back of the building seemed well protected from wandering eyes.

"No windows on the street level. Two entrances. Second floor holds what? Meeting room, offices, sleeping areas?" Norm talked to himself, trying to make sense of the building, knowing what he did about the people who would be inside.

"What does it matter? The back door looks like the main entrance." I wanted him to know I listened and had ideas of my own.

"You come in the front they know you're not one of the members," Norm said. "Upstairs matters, because it's an unknown and unknowns have a tendency to bite you in the ass when you ain't lookin'."

"Good point, Norm, but who's planning on going inside? We wait for Morgan to show himself outside and we follow him. I didn't notice an opening time posted anywhere, so how do we schedule surveillance?"

"Probably always open for some." Norm drove, making turns as the lady in the GPS told him to. "I think because of the strippers, the club has regular hours. Maybe nine to whatever or later. It doesn't say it's a private club so it should be open to the public. Technically. "

"Why's that matter?"

"How'd they get a liquor license?" Norm turned onto route 40 west toward Aston when the GPS told him to.

"Someone's clean, no criminal record. It happens a lot. They get the license. Maybe an attorney or a trust." I'd seen it in Los Angeles and other cities. Gangster Whitey Bulger owned a liquor store in South Boston, but in someone else's name.

"Worth looking into how the agency missed all this." Norm sped along not much over the speed limit thinking about his agency that had its eye on everyone and its sudden lack of available information. "I'm guessing the businesses around there are closed by nine. That should make finding a spot to do surveillance easier. I'd be surprised if they didn't have some sort of perimeter security. We need to watch for that."

"You're giving them a lot of credit." Did Norm know something he hadn't shared or did he treat this as one of his military operations?

Roadside businesses on route 40 gave way to a forest and a four-lane roadway to two lanes, except where passing came and went quickly. Signs indicated the road had Florida Highway Patrol and local sheriffs policing it. We never saw any. What we assumed were dirt fire roads appeared randomly on both sides of route 40, as did rural mailboxes, indicating a residence or a campground.

Campground signs hyped cabins but all we could see through the trees were small trailers. What most locations had in common were waterfronts that offered boating, fishing and hiking on either a lake or river.

Soon after the Lake George State Forest sign, we arrived in Astor. A drawbridge spanned the wide Saint John's River and the steel grating of the bridge rattled as vehicles drover over it. Semi tractor-trailers seemed to drag the noise out and certainly made it louder.

On the left hand side, after the bridge, we pulled into the Astor Marina Lodge. Late afternoon and the North Florida weather had turned chilly. Norm and I wore jackets that concealed our handguns and kept us warm. Padre Thomas had put on a sweater and long pants in Daytona.

Off the large, almost empty parking lot, the marina's motel rooms lined up in front of boat slips, offering guests a view of the river. Many of the boats were 20-plus foot cabin cruisers. A few small sailboats bobbed in the water. The fast-moving river looked wide enough to make sailing enjoyable.

The two-story waterfront building housed a small marina office and large restaurant on the first floor. The second story held a ship's store and two offices, according to the directory next to the stairway.

We took a seat on the restaurant's outside deck, a large barge platform with round tables and chairs, that rocked from waves as boats sped by. The sun behind the building sparkled on the river but the structure kept it from shining on us.

We ordered our lunch and coffee from a waitress whose nametag said she was Annamae, hoping the coffee would keep us warm as we waited for the others.

"Nice boats." Norm accepted his coffee cup and held it in both hands.

Padre Thomas and I added sugar and milk to ours, as close as we'd get to *café con leche* in Astor.

"Good for going unnoticed if you were transporting something illegal." Norm sipped his coffee. He opened the paper map and we both looked at our location. "Homes and whatever, more campgrounds to the north." He ran a finger along the river. "South there seems to be a lot of forest between the river and route 17."

"More desolate on the west side of the river," I said. "Fire roads a few miles up may go into that area."

When Annamae came to take our plates Norm smiled. "Does anyone rent boats here?"

"Sure enough." She smiled back. "See Griff down on the dock. He's a grouchy old codger, so watch him. He barks a lot but his teeth got knocked out a long time ago, so he's got no bite. This late in the afternoon, he should give you a deal. Be dark by six."

"Thank you."

Annamae took the dishes away and brought us fresh coffee. "What are you boys going out on the water so late for?"

"Check out the river a little and see if we should come back tomorrow," Norm said.

"What's south of here?" I said.

"Lake Dexter," she said. "Fishin', swimin', if that's your thing."

"Any old fishin' camps or maybe deserted campgrounds close by?" I said. "I do a lot of nature photography and old becomes rustic in my world."

She thought for a minute. "On the west side of the river, 'bout a couple of miles down there's these ruins of what people say was a rich man's fishin' camp back in the early 1900s." Annamae blushed. "Used to go there to neck when I was in high school," she said. "Got the grandkids to prove it, too. Suppose today the kids still do."

"Will we see the ruins from the water?" Norm said.

"No. Everything's grown over these days." Annamae's blush had gone. "Couple of years ago, I was down river with a friend in his boat. We joked about the old camp and I think it was opposite where lightning had cut a tree in half. Hard to miss, all the other trees are huge. I'm not positive 'bout the location."

"Thanks, Annamae, you've been a help." Norm accepted the bill and handed it to me.

Pauly pulled into the parking lot as we exited the restaurant.

"Burt's a couple of minutes behind me," Pauly said as he and Bob got out. "Anything?"

Padre Thomas stayed close, but not close enough to interfere as Norm and I brought them up to date. Halfway through, Burt and Texas Rich arrived.

They reported no motorcycle sightings other than the two earlier but they wore helmets and not gang clothing.

"We stopped for lunch and then again maybe an hour away, at roadside diners," Pauly said. "Asked about bikers because there were signs outside the places welcoming them. Weekend bikers, they said. Riding the country road. No Hells Angels, as one bartender called them."

Norm spread his map out on a picnic table and showed everyone where Annamae thought there'd be the ruins of an old fishing camp.

"Okay," Pauly said. "Makes sense that Bob and I rent the boat, do a quick recon and get back before night."

"Why does it make sense?" Norm said. Maybe seriously wondering why or maybe a dig at Pauly.

"Bob and I are water people," Pauly said. "We've got our sea legs. We'll see what we can see from the water and be back here in a couple of hours. Tomorrow we can use the whole day, but now it's wham-bam-thank-you-ma'am time."

First, we had to deal with a temperamental old codger named Griff.

On the Water
Chapter EIGHTEEN

Griff wasn't hard to find. An old man with a worn pipe clenched between his yellowed teeth, thick white smoke from its bowl wafting away in the cold breeze. He sat alone on the dock and focused on the river like most of us watch television. Stained overalls strapped atop a long-sleeved work shirt, ratty sneakers held together in places with duct tape. I knew if the dictionary had a photo next to the word *codger*, it would be Griff's. In need of a shave and haircut, spikes of white hair sprouted along his ears. Glasses poked out of an overall pocket, the other top pocket looked stuffed with a tobacco pouch and pipe cleaners.

"Griff?" Pauly extended his hand.

"Who's askin'?" He stayed seated, ignoring Pauly's hand.

"Annamae told us you rented boats." Pauly brought his hand back.

"Yup." Griff pulled a pocket watch from his overalls, looked at it and returned it. "Late to be goin' on the water."

"Want to look around, see if we'll come back tomorrow," Pauly said.

Griff looked at each of us. "What kind of boat you boys lookin' to rent?"

"Something for only two of us now," Pauly said. "A quick run south to check it out. Be back before sunset."

"Done cleaned and stowed everything." Griff got up, tapped his pipe on the ground, gray and black ash spilled out. "Gonna have to charge you full rate."

"How much?" Norm said.

Griff scratched at his beard stubble. "Two hundred. I'm givin' you a break 'cause a day's rate is two-fifty. You'll rent from me tomorrow, too, right?"

Pauly handed Griff his credit card. "You're a silver

tongued devil, Griff."

Griff scratched his neck and smiled. "Be right back." He hobbled toward the restaurant.

When Pauly had signed the credit card form, Griff walked us to a nineteen-foot Boston Whaler, suitable for eight. He checked his pocket watch, again.

"Be dark by six." He returned the watch. "If I have to stay till dark, there's an extra charge."

"Be back at five-thirty." Pauly started the engine as Bob untied the lines.

"We'll need a boat for all of us tomorrow." I looked toward the slipped cabin cruisers. "Any of them rentals?"

"Nope." Griff filled and lit his pipe with wooden matches, cupping his hands to keep the wind away. "I got one." He limped to his chair and sat, ignoring us.

Padre Thomas went to the Jeep. Burt and Texas Rich spent a little time telling us how nothing happened on the ride from Ocala and then walked to the restaurant. Norm and I strolled along the wooden dock, looking at boats, all the while under Griff's watchful gaze.

A little before four, Pauly called. I put the phone on speaker and Norm and I leaned against a piling. "Annamae called it. Half hour south. Close to the damaged tree is a creek and we can see a boat a ways in there."

"Any activity? Can you see the old fish camp building?" Norm said.

"Nothing." Pauly sounded disappointed. "We're goin' up the creek."

"Might not be a good idea," Norm said. "If it's the Rattlers they probably have someone watching the river."

"We won't confront anyone," Bob said.

"We'll be back before five-thirty." Pauly disconnected the call.

Norm stared south to where Pauly and Bob were. "It's someone confronting them that worries me."

After twenty minutes passed, I called Pauly every five minutes for the next fifteen minutes. His phone went right to message. Norm or I wouldn't have been concerned, if Pauly hadn't said he was going up the creek. Without saying, we both knew something wasn't right.

"I think our friends are lost or have engine problems," I said as Norm and I approached Griff.

"Not engine problems," Griff said. "You want me to go look for 'em? It costs extra."

"We'll go," Norm said.

Griff checked his pocket watch. "Gettin' late."

I handed him a credit card. "Put another Whaler on it and leave it open for tomorrow."

Griff smirked. "The other guy's credit card is open for tomorrow and in case he comes back late." He handed me my card. "I'll just add your costs to it."

Griff led us to another nineteen-foot Whaler. The keys were in the ignition.

"You boys know how to use the radio?" He untied our lines.

"Of course." I started the engine.

"You need help, call me on channel sixteen."

"You'll come?" He surprised me.

"Come for my boats." He shuffled off toward the restaurant.

The sun sat low in the sky. It would be dusk soon and night within an hour.

Shadows filled the river and woods. A strong current pushed the Whaler along until I had the 150-horse powered engine running. We sped along. I found the switch for the running lights, but I left them off. I didn't want to be too visible from the shore as darkness arrived. In twenty minutes, Norm had me slow and we both scanned the shadows for the lightning-struck tree stump.

"There! Two o'clock!" Norm pointed ahead, using the

numeral locations on a clock so I'd look in the right direction.

The current pushed us past the location. I turned the boat and kept the throttle to where the boat only crept forward against the current. As we passed the creek, we could see two boats tied off, maybe 50 yards in.

"How soggy do you think the ground is?" Norm said.

"Not the faintest," I said.

"Fuck the boat," he said. "Run into the woods until we hit solid ground."

I turned north of the creek and slowly worked the bow of the Whaler through brush, tilting the motor up to keep it from hitting the bottom. Most of the overhanging branches scraped the sides and scratched the windshield. We edged along, pushing tree limbs out of our faces. I kept the engine as low as possible until the boat jerked to a stop and the engine revved.

Quickly, I shut it off, not wanting to advertise our arrival. Norm grabbed the bowline and tied it off to a tree.

"Can we get out from here?" He said. "If we're in a hurry?"

I shook my head. "Carefully." I followed him into the ankle-high water.

The muddy ground made the going slow, but that worked for us because Norm felt certain the Rattlers would have security. We moved forward, not talking, our guns in hand. Shadows got darker. The ground became more solid.

Norm grabbed my shoulder when we were across from the Whaler Pauly and Bob had come on. "Smell that?"

"How could you avoid it," I said. The air held a hint of what smelled like wet paint drying and rotting garbage. Not overbearing, but getting there.

"They're cooking meth," he said. "Gotta be them."

The creek became narrow and, a few hundred feet from us, we could see a clearing, but no cabin or remnants of one.

Moving between the trees, we pushed forward, staying away from the clearing.

Unrecognizable voices filtered through the forest. We stopped. It wasn't Pauly or Bob talking.

Keeping the clearing to our left, we continued forward, measuring each step, avoiding broken branches and looking for trip wires.

When we were at the far end of the clearing, we turned and moved toward it, hiding behind the biggest trees and clumps of bushes available.

A stone fire pit took up the center of the area and had chairs around it. There was no fire burning. Three men stood there holding military assault rifles.

Kneeling on the ground, hands behind their heads were Pauly and Bob.

Norm's Plan
Chapter NINETEEN

Norm placed his hand over my mouth as I began to say something. His eyes looked hard at me and he shook his head. I knew the look from past misadventures. It meant shut up, and listen. We backed up a few yards and crouched behind an undergrowth of bushes.

"Three of them," Norm whispered, even though we could no longer hear muffled talk from the clearing. "Has to be more wherever the lab is."

"We need to do something!" I wanted to shout about helping Bob and Pauly before someone put a bullet in their heads. "That doesn't look good, them kneeling there."

"I got a plan," Norm said. "You follow it and if Bob's SEAL training kicks in we may get out of this."

He told me his plan. It put me in immediate danger and its success depended as much on Norm's black-bag skills as Bob's knowing when to react. The choices were few and none of them good.

We retraced our steps to the boat and pushed it out to where I could lower the engine tilt enough to start it in the water.

"Give me five minutes to get in place," Norm said.

"That going to be enough time?"

"It's how much time Bob and Pauly have left that concerns me." Norm backed off. "Five minutes, hoss." He got to dry ground, crouched and began to sprint into the woods.

I started the engine and backed up. As soon as the current caught the boat, I let it take me past the damaged stump and then turned into the current and brought the horsepower up enough to keep the boat fighting the current but not moving with it.

The sun no longer sparkled on the water and only a highlighting of it showed low from behind the woods to the west. Enough glimmer to keep the sky from turning black. The temperature had dropped enough for me to see my breath. If nothing else, it reminded me we were no longer in Key West. I looked up the creek and the two boats were in deep shadows. Almost invisible.

My eyes stayed focused on my wristwatch. How could Norm covertly make the distance through the woods with nature's debris scattered in the way? If he judged wrong, I would be kneeling next to Bob and Pauly within minutes.

At five-eighteen, I turned the Whaler toward the creek and drove to the other boats. The creek's width allowed enough turning room, so I maneuvered the boat and pointed the bow toward the river. By the time I tied off to the back of the other rental boat, my engine tilt was as high as it could go and the Whaler had scraped the bottom of the creek.

I climbed over the other two boats, found the keys to the cabin cruiser in the ignition, and tossed them into the water. I dropped off the side of the boat and hit dry ground. My Sig rested in my jacket pocket, ready to shoot, if it came to that. I took deep breaths as I walked but the anxiety I felt stayed. I lied to myself by thinking the scenario of why I searched for the owner of a skiff that hit my boat would cause me to be upset and nervous. I needed to be believable, for a short while anyway. My life and the lives of my friends depended on it.

My vision diminished as the sun set. The air got cooler. Maybe I could see twenty feet. For how long, I wasn't sure. Voices, soft with laughter, came through the darkness.

Show time.

"Hey! Hey! Someone out there?" I yelled, slowing my pace. "One of the boats lost its skiff and it damaged my boat! Hey! Who's there?"

I walked toward the darkness. The voices ceased.

The Sig felt cold and reassuring in my hand, even in my pocket. Yelling to get the bikers' attention on me and off their surroundings, I moved through the heavy shadows, wanting my movements to be loud and distracting.

Five feet from the clearing, one man stood, his assault rifle aimed at me.

"Whoa! Buddy. I'm only looking for whoever owns the skiff." I stopped and fought the urge to raise my hands. "I don't want any trouble." My finger moved to the Sig's trigger.

He motioned me forward with the rifle.

Bob and Pauly remained kneeling, hands still on their heads. They didn't look toward me. Two others with rifles stood close to the fire pit.

"What are you doing here?" The biker looked out of central casting in Hollywood. Santa Claus beard, but it was a natty brown not white, denim pants and jacket, no shirt to cover his beer belly. Tattoos ran up and down his arms.

Pointing behind me I said, "The skiff from one of those boats broke away and hit my boat. Only a scratch, but I wanted to let someone know." I kept my voice low so they would focus on me. "Skiff's tied off to my boat." I pointed behind me again. "I can show you."

"You know these guys?" The man that met me said. "You from Key West?"

"I'm camping up there," I pointed north, hoping the bikers' stare would follow, "with my wife and kids. We're visiting from Boston."

The three of them looked at each other. They huddled and whispered. Norm inched up behind them, a large tree limb in his hands.

"Look it," I said to draw their attention to me. "I'll tie the skiff off to one of the boats and go. I'm not interested in your feud. I just want to get back to the wife and kids." I began to turn and move to get their attention focused on me.

Norm moved up, the limb held high and he brought it down hard, quickly hitting each biker high on the shoulders and back of the neck. The swing blurred and the bikers bent over with a surprised look on their faces, but didn't go down. Bob tackled one and I brought my Sig out as Norm knocked one to the ground and then pressed his gun against the ear of the last man standing.

Pauly and Bob took the assault rifles from the men.

"You had to go up the creek!" Norm said to Pauly, shaking his head. "How many others?"

"One took our wallets and headed that way." Pauly pointed behind Norm. "Wherever that smell's coming from, there must be others."

"How many others?" Norm hit the biker behind the ear with the barrel of his gun. "How many?"

"You'll know soon enough, asshole!" The biker spat the words.

Norm screwed a suppressor onto the barrel of his semi-automatic. He grabbed the earring in the man's ear and pulled. "You won't be here to see it asshole!" Norm pulled the earring from the man's ear, causing him to yelp in pain and reach for his torn ear. "How many?"

"Fuck you!"

Norm pressed the tip of the suppressor against the man's head and pulled the trigger. The man crumpled to the ground, the left side of his head, along with brain matter splattering on his two cohorts.

"Anyone else want me to pull their earring?" Norm snarled at the two bikers as they tried to wipe the bloody carnage from their faces.

Bob and Pauly retrieved their handguns from the two men.

"Their buddy took our wallets." Pauly checked his gun. "They saw we came from Key West and got all excited."

"You know Morgan Pryce?" Norm placed the suppressor

against the biker's ear.

He nodded.

"Is he here?" The length of the suppressor hit the man's head.

He shook his head. The Rattler's denim uniform looked old and dirty. His soiled hair in a long ponytail, tats and the beginning of the beer belly, all indications of a loser biker.

"Where is he?" Norm focused his attention on the next man.

Bob tapped Norm on the shoulder, a silence passed between them and Bob headed toward the meth lab.

"Where?" Norm said.

"Daytona," the other man said. "If I were you, I'd move because there's a lot more of us coming."

"Not without our wallets," Pauly said.

Norm pushed the talker backward. "How many more?"

"You don't have enough ammo," the man said.

He looked younger than the other man did, and a lot more alive than the dead biker. He probably wanted to stay that way.

"You can't stand up to the firepower, either," he said as Norm pushed him further back.

Bob came back leading another potbellied, bearded biker. You needed a scorecard with photos to tell them apart. Like so many groups that tout their individuality, the Rattlers dressed in a uniform that identified them wherever they went. They made themselves easy targets for law enforcement.

Each of us now had an assault rifle, but no extra magazines.

"No wallets." Bob hit the biker on the back of the head. He looked at the dead man and then turned to Norm. He shook his head.

"No wallets! Shit!" Pauly said. "I'm fucked without it. No credit cards, no ID . . ."

"Kept them at the cabin, right?" He wacked the biker on the side of the head with his Kimber 1911 semi-automatic.

The biker only nodded.

"Down to the boat," Norm said to the bikers. "If you'd rather join your friend, say so now."

The three bikers walked ahead and stopped at the boat.

"Disable the engine," Norm said to Bob. "Pauly, find something we can tie these three up with."

Pauly came back with a short roll of wire. He led the men onto the boat deck and began binding their hands behind their backs.

"Morgan might not know Pauly or Bob by name," I said to Norm. "But two Key West guys showing up, both with handguns ..."

"Yeah," Norm said. "We've lost the element of surprise."

Trapped on the Water
Chapter TWENTY

The first salvos caught us by surprise. Bullets came in high and tore into the top of the cruiser's cabin so violently that the boat rocked. Barrel flashes lit up the darkness in the forest and the explosive reports sent birds scurrying into the night air. We dropped and lowered ourselves into the cockpit.

"That was fast!" Pauly yelled, as bullets flew over our heads, some puncturing the side of the boat.

We had no idea of how many Rattlers shot at us, but from the number of holes ripped through the boat, there were a few of them.

"Christ! They're shooting automatic weapons." Norm listened to the rapid rounds as he readied his assault rifle. "They've gotta change magazines. That will give us a few seconds when they do it."

"A few seconds to do what?" I said.

"You and Mick get going, cut loose the line tying us together and then I can back the Whaler out with Bob's help." Pauly spoke to Norm as he crouched by the engines.

The shooting slowed. Looking over the gunwale, I saw six barrel flashes as shots came at us.

"I'm tied to your Whaler, bow forward, headed to the river." I slid over to the cabin's hatchway. "If I can get over there, I could pull you out. Backing up is tricky, you know that Pauly, and the creek is shallow. You run aground, you're done."

"How you gonna get two boats over?" Norm said. "These guys are ex-military. Someone in charge knows what he's doing."

"We've got four assault rifles, shoot back, cover me," I said.

"I can swim that distance underwater," Bob said. "Not a problem."

"I'm tied off to one aft cleat," I said. "We need to tie off to one more, so I can pull you out straight."

"I can pull the boat forward," Bob said. "All you need to do is get over in it."

"You get as high as the rail and you're a clear target." Norm pointed at the gunwale. "Don't know if they've got a sniper out there."

"Cover me, like Mick said. We got assault rifles, fire back." Bob stared at the distance he needed to cover. A chilled air caused the creek's warm water to mist. "You got the keys?"

The windscreen shattered with the next volley of shots. The boat kept swaying.

"Bad news is they're probably sending guys to the other side of the river. Get us in a cross fire," Norm said.

"Now or never." I slid the boat's key to Bob.

Norm held his hand up, stopping Bob.

"Watch the other side for movement." Norm moved Pauly to the creek side of the boat. "Don't shoot unless you can hit someone. All we have is a magazine each."

Norm pointed for me to shoot from the gunwale as he kneeled behind the cabin.

"Shoot single shots, Mick," he said. "These are automatics and will empty the magazine in seconds." Norm turned to Pauly. "Don't shoot until you see a muzzle flash."

Pauly nodded.

Norm turned to Bob. "As soon as we start."

Bob nodded.

In the darkness, the bikers remained unseen. The shooting had stopped. The blackness meant Bob should be able to drop over the rail into the water without notice. Across the creek, nightfall hid everything. No shadows of trees. No movement of men. The sky above held a plethora of stars, but no moon yet. A soft mist hugged the river and crept along the side of the boat.

"Single shots to draw them out, Mick." Norm looked at Bob and repeated himself. "As soon as you hear us shoot."

Bob nodded. "When you hear the engine start, I'll be ready to go."

"In five," Norm said and counted.

When he said five, he fired a couple of random shots into the darkness. I did the same and within seconds, the bikers returned fire. Bob went over the rail and I didn't hear him splash into the water.

Another long barrage tore into the landside gunwale. Norm fell back. I shot toward the muzzle flashes.

"You okay?" The shooting stopped. I crawled to Norm.

"Yeah, winged my shoulder, is all." Norm sat up. "Listen!" Stillness surrounded us.

"The shooting stopped," Pauly said.

"A motor," Norm said. "It's getting louder. Listen."

"Another boat?" I looked toward the river.

"Afraid so," Norm said. "No running lights. Moving cautiously."

"Maybe Bob can sneak up on it?" I said.

"I hear it!" Pauly looked toward the river. "Don't see shit."

"They'll have us surrounded as soon as the boat gets close," Norm said. "Bob's on the first boat. We need to make a run for it and get the hell out of here. Jump from boat to boat and hope Bob doesn't shoot us. Ready?"

Pauly and I nodded.

The Getaway
Chapter TWENTY-ONE

A fusillade came from across the river. The muzzle flashes appeared as distant circles of light, like fireflies swarming in the night. Their loud report swallowed in the night's cold breeze. Pauly fired two shots toward them.

"Save your ammo," Norm said. "We gotta make this fast."

Our dash would be at least twenty-five feet across an open, pitching boat, considering the length of the first boat and the water distance between it and Bob's boat. The night might hide us, or at least the first person across. Once the Rattlers began firing we would be moving in unprotected area, targeted from both sides and from the oncoming boat. There was little any of us could do to protect ourselves. A half-moon had risen, and with the night sky full of stars, replaced the protective darkness with murkiness that would expose us as shadowy images as we ran. A mist continued blanketing the creek.

We sat on the cockpit floor, our backs against the cabin.

"Leave me the rifles," Norm said, his warm breath steaming in the cold air. "I'll shoot over the bow toward land and Mick you start moving, then Pauly. Their fire should be focused on where the shots came from."

"And when I'm over, who covers you?" Pauly said.

"I'll get the last shots off," Norm said, "and when they return fire, I'll run like hell."

"After Mick crosses, they'll know we're moving," Pauly said. "You'll be an easy target they're ready for."

"What about the water?" I said after a moment. "Couldn't we go off the side and swim, hide in the darkness?"

Engine sounds crept closer. More shots came from across the river, rocking the boat.

"We'll be easy pickings for whoever's on that boat," Norm said. "We'd be unable to defend ourselves."

"Better than leaving you here." I looked toward Pauly and he nodded. "Swim toward Bob."

"Thought you hated cold water." Norm grinned at me, remembering times I wore a wetsuit in Southern California's cold water and he tormented me for it.

"When given the choice, which I'm not at the moment," I said. "Yeah."

The boat engine's low-gear growl grew louder.

"Another option." Norm stared into the darkness from where the rumble came. "We attack the boat, kill the bastards on board and use it to get the hell out of here. If that fails, we can swim for it."

"It might give us a few seconds of confusion. What do they shoot at from across the river? Might hit their own men." Pauly ejected the rifle's magazine and counted the bullets. "Twenty-two left."

Norm had fifteen bullets and I had twenty.

"Bob has his 1911, he might figure out what we're doing and come for us," Norm said. "That Kimber .45 would be helpful."

"Let's do it!" Pauly's enthusiasm embarrassed me because everything happening sent tremors through me.

"We've gotta stick behind the gunwale," Norm said. "Mick, down by the engines. Pauly, by the cabin and me in the middle."

The cockpit was less than twenty-feet long, with a ten-foot beam that put us close together and offered the only protection we had. We took our places. I wondered how smart it was to ignore the bikers on the landside of us, but squeezed in between the engine and gunwale.

"Shoot at someone, not the night," Norm said as the boat's shadow appeared. "And hope Bob comes for us."

Crouched in place, I watched the gray shadow of the

boat's bow creep out of the darkness. The misty black river seemed to be giving birth as the boat steadily emerged like a newborn. Slowly, the engine cries grew louder and closer as more of the boat's shadow appeared.

The silhouettes of one man standing at the helm, two at the stern, came into view. Easy targets as they moved closer to our boat. The man on the starboard side held a line, as if he was prepared to toss it.

"Norm," I said as low as I could and still be heard.

"See it," he said.

Pauly slipped away from his position and went into the bullet-raked cabin. He came back with a flash light.

"Three guys below, lying on the floor but okay." After reporting on the hogtied bikers below deck, Pauly got back in position. "I'll turn this on the helm, you take him out, Norm."

"Hold on," Norm said as we watched the open boat approach. "Shine it on the stern, the guy with the line."

Pauly turned on the light and pointed at the man holding the line.

"Off!" Norm shouted when he recognized Bob. Gunshots came from across the creek, aimed at the moving boat.

Bob stood on the stern, ready to toss us a line so we could pull the boat close enough for us to board. Burt waved from the helm and Texas Rich returned the gunfire using one of Pauly's M4s. I grabbed the line, when Bob tossed it, and pulled the boat close. We jumped on board, Burt put the engine in reverse and we idled at our rental Whaler.

Shots from both sides of the creek smacked into the water less than ten feet away from us.

"You want to bring 'em back?" Bob said. "All tied off. All I need to do is cut the aft line to the cruiser."

"I'll do it." Pauly jumped onto my Whaler, followed by Bob who went onto the boat he'd come in. "Go!" Pauly put the engine into gear and towed the second boat behind us.

Once in the Saint Johns River the running lights on all three boats came on. Bob cut loose from Pauly, turned the boat around and we rushed up-river to the marina.

Texas Rich, Norm and I stood close to Burt at the helm, watching the distant lights of the marinas grow brighter.

"How'd you find us?" I said.

"Padre Thomas came for us about half an hour after you left," Burt said. "Told us you were in trouble and called in your location."

"Shit, you shouldn't have left without us," Texas Rich said.

"Pauly wasn't supposed to make contact," Norm growled.

"When does Pauly every follow directions?" Texas Rich said. "He'll get us killed."

"Glad you got hold of the dock master and Padre Thomas," Burt said.

"I am too." I looked at Norm and we both knew we hadn't made any call.

Norm shook his head and I knew he didn't want to talk about it. Not now, not ever.

I nodded my agreement but knew he was becoming a believer in the angels. It sometimes became hard not to.

"Now what?" Burt moved the Whaler into a slip.

"We have a strip club in Daytona to visit." Norm tapped my shoulder and pointed at Griff. "I'm glad it's Pauly's credit card and not mine."

Griff sauntered down the dock, a scowl on his face. Or maybe that was his way of smiling.

A Cartoon Character in Dirty Overalls
Chapter TWENTY-TWO

Lights along the dock highlighted each slip, removing the river's long, cold shadows from us. Griff looked at all three Whalers without saying anything. He bent down, touched the scratches and bullet holes in the hulls, and looked inside the open cockpits while we waited on the dock. Finally, he stood and gave us each a hard stare while shaking his head as if preparing to chastise a child.

"This one," he looked toward me, "got hacked up pretty good by the bushes. Suppose it ran aground too. Gotta check below the waterline." Griff scratched at his beard stubble. "Holes in this one." He looked at Pauly. "Don't suppose you know how that happened?"

Pauly shook his head. "We hit some rough waves from bigger boats. Our wallets went overboard."

"Not an explanation." Griff frowned. "Why's there so many holes in your boat?" He looked at Burt, who hunched his shoulders in silent reply. "Lucky Whalers don't sink. Got 'em as rentals for clowns like you bandits."

Griff took his pipe out of his overalls, filled it, then turned his back to the cold breeze to light it. "Lot of fireworks earlier." He exhaled smoke that mixed with the frost of his breath. "How senile do you boys think I am?"

Our breath steamed into the night but no words followed.

"Gonna have to charge you ten thousand for the repairs." Griff waited for a reply, received none and then looked at Pauly. "That go down okay with you?"

"Sounds about right," Pauly said. "I'm going to report my credit cards lost, so I'm not sure how that'll work."

"It will work just fine, son," Griff said. "I'm gonna put the final charge on the card now and when you report it lost, you tell 'em the charges from the Astor Marina are good."

"I can do that," Pauly said.

"Wouldn't think of cheating me, afterward, would you?" Griff bit down on the pipe's stem.

"Not a cheater, when it's honest payment," Pauly said.

Griff talked with the pipe clenched between his teeth and nodded his understanding. "Y'all don't look like bikers." He circled around us, humming to himself. "Don't act like lawmen." He stopped under a light, looking like a cartoon character, in his dirty overalls and clenched pipe. "What are y'all?"

I didn't know how to answer Griff. He obviously knew more than he gave away and his hick appearance and talk hid intelligence. Eventually, we all stared at Norm and Griff noticed.

"Well, boss man, with muddy cowboy boots, looks like y'all been elected." Griff walked a few steps closer to Norm, but stayed more than an arm's length away.

Norm gave Griff one of his smiles that are more hostile than welcoming. "For an old coot, you don't miss much."

"Thank you." Griff waited for more.

"You know what's going on up the river?" Norm kept the smile. Griff kept silent. "We're looking for someone and believe him to be with the bikers."

Griff knocked the ashes from his pipe onto the dock.

"There's a reward on him," Norm said when Griff didn't reply. "Think of us as bounty hunters."

Griff didn't react to Norm's explanation. I expected him to. He scratched at the stubble on his neck and looked toward the drawbridge.

"The bikers gonna come here lookin' for y'all." Griff gave a glance at the rifle Texas Rich held. "I don't need no trouble, so y'all better go."

"You be okay?" Norm, too, looked toward the drawbridge.

For the first time, we heard Griff laugh. "They got the

numbers, but they're potbellied fools. No matter. I ain't afraid of 'em. Not sure what kind of drugs they're doing up there, and don't wanna know, but they don't want the cops here snooping around. Better to leave us alone. If I was y'all, I'd be careful on the road."

"They'll want to know about us," Norm said. "They've got the wallets of these two." He pointed at Pauly and Bob.

"I can only tell 'em what I know," Griff said. "He rented one boat, paid for all three." He nodded toward Pauly. "Don't know where y'all come from or where y'all goin'. Tell 'em the truth."

"We'll be in touch," Norm said as we walked off the dock.

"Don't do me no favors." Griff limped toward the dark restaurant without looking at us and maybe still laughing.

"Convoy?" Burt opened the door to his truck.

Texas Rich kept the M4 with him.

"Yeah," Norm said. "Follow me to the hotel."

"What about the bikers?" Pauly stood by his Jeep. "We've got the firepower now to take them on." He held up his duffel bag of weapons reminding us he'd left a similar one with each vehicle.

"We don't want to take on the Rattlers." I restated. "We want Morgan and he's not with them."

"You believe the guy?" Pauly sounded surprised.

"Yeah," Norm said. "He's a cop."

"Who's a cop?" Bob said.

"How do you know?" Pauly said.

"The way he answered my questions," Norm said. "He was telling me there are a lot of bikers at the cabin and they're well armed He was telling us to get the hell out of there while we could."

"You sure?" I sat in the Jeep. Padre Thomas slept in back.

"Yeah, it's what you say when you don't answer the question that's important, especially if you're undercover,"

Norm said. "Which kind of makes me wonder whose undercover cop he is?"

"Does it matter?" Bob started his truck.

"Sure does." Norm got in the Jeep, gave a quick glance toward Padre Thomas. "We're stepping on someone's toes and since we don't have law enforcement backing us, they'll think we're Rattler's competitors. Trying to keep them out of our meth business area."

"Can't you fix it with a call, or something?" Texas Rich said.

"Possibly, later. Not now. I need to know more." Norm started the Jeep.

"You mean they'll think we're meth dealers?" The thought surprised me.

"Or worse."

"What's worse?" Padre Thomas sat up, yawning.

Breakfast and the Feds
Chapter TWENTY-THREE

Eastbound along route 40, we dealt with only a few cars and trucks on the road. Westbound, small packs of speeding bikers headed to Astor. The late night hour kept us from seeing if they were Rattler reinforcements or not. As long as they headed west, I didn't really care. It meant fewer bikers at the Tit-4-Tat.

Soon after we drove under I-95, the woman in the GPS had us turn right and we traveled on streets with cinderblock business centers until she instructed Norm to turn left into residential neighborhoods that finally led to our hotel in Daytona. Traffic on the side streets caused the trip to be a little more than one hour.

Norm kept quiet and I figured he didn't want to talk about what happened with Padre Thomas in the back seat. It worked for me because I didn't want to give too much thought to Norm shooting the biker in cold blood. I knew that his job sometimes called for the assassination of drug lords and other cartel members, but I had never witnessed it. If the shooting bothered him, he hid it well. I thought of him more as a sniper than an up-close and personal assassin. We'd been in gun battles before and people died, but I always considered it self-defense. I would have to rethink all that, now.

Pauly, Bob, Norm and I were dirty from our escapade in the woods and on the river, and went to our rooms to clean up. Padre Thomas stayed awake and waited in my room. Burt and Texas Rich went in search of a restaurant that offered takeout, as long as it wasn't a fast food burger joint.

Norm had the hotel's only mini-suite, so we gathered there and scarfed down the warm pizza Burt and Texas Rich brought back. They also found a twelve pack of Bohemia, a dark Mexican beer. Comfort food after what we'd gone through.

When we'd all had our two-cents worth of rehashing the evening, and the pizza was eaten, there remained little doubt that we couldn't have handled the situation any differently. Once Pauly took the boat up the creek, we'd lost control. Norm smiled when he reminded us of that. We admitted that the outcome might have been different if Padre Thomas hadn't told Burt and Texas Rich about our phone call and location.

Norm and I avoided looking at Padre Thomas. He kept quiet, eating his pizza and wishing he had a Budweiser. His lie stayed between us.

We were tired. The drive, the shoot-out, it had all taken a toll on us, but we agreed a quick night-run by the Tit-4-Tat couldn't be avoided. How the club functioned when open would help us determine how best to snatch Morgan. No one thought the back parking lot would be the best place to take Morgan, but it would serve well for locating him and beginning the chase.

Eleven at night and the strip club's back lot looked half-filled. Or, if you preferred, half-empty. Music and laughter blared out whenever the double doors opened. No one parked out front and no one went in the back lot who didn't drive in on a Hog.

The alleyway of the strip mall behind the Tit-4-Tat gave us a dark location and clear view of the club's poorly lit lot. Morgan's Clydesdale size would be the only way we could identify him from our vantage point. The bikers tended to be large, but much of it had to do with beer bellies and scruffy beards. Morgan kept in shape and hadn't had time to grow a beard. His size and shape would betray him, and help us.

* * *

Six hours sleep and in-room coffee did little to satisfy me.

By seven-thirty, everyone wanted breakfast. Norm found a diner via Google and we drove across the high bridge on International Speedway Boulevard and into Daytona Beach. The old-fashioned diner looked small from the outside, but once inside I realized it ran deep. Seating for 20 at the oval counter in front; booths and tables filled the rest of the diner, and the satisfying aroma of bacon grease, frying eggs and strong, hot coffee, wafted through the air.

Celicia, according to her nametag, an attractive waitress, led us to the largest booth in the diner. We sat in the back, far from the entrance and the busy counter.

Our food tastes varied and we told Celicia to bring the individual orders as done and not to wait to bring it all at once. She smiled her thanks and poured our coffee.

"After yesterday, do you think Morgan's on the run again?" Bob spoke it as an open question.

"Do you think they know we're looking for him?" I turned to Norm, he had the experience in this kind of search and seizure game.

"They know Bob and Pauly are from Key West." Norm's sarcasm went directly to Pauly who took the path that led to the confrontation. "If Morgan doesn't know them, the bikers might think it's a coincidence."

"What else could it be?" Burt said.

"Two guys from the Keys, escaping the hot weather. Drug smugglers wanting to branch out," Norm said. "I want to assume that the undercover agent didn't report that we questioned him on Morgan."

"The dead bikcr kind of takes us away from the escaping hot weather scenario," Bob said.

"There's that." Norm nodded his agreement. "The best thing in this situation is to expect the worst."

"And that is what?" Burt said.

"That would depend on the answers we don't have to our questions." Norm looked around the table. "It could be we're looking for Morgan or we want in on their meth operation or we want to stop them from cutting in on our meth operation."

"It's too soon for them to be coordinating Morgan's blackmail scheme. It hasn't been enough time for their bosses to really consider it." I thought about these things last night, trying to figure where we stood and what the bikers would be looking for.

"I agree," Norm said. "If we take that off the table what's it leave us?"

"It has to do with the meth operation," Pauly said. "They're moving in on us or we want in with them."

"Right," Norm said.

The food came in one order. The kitchen staff either had a slow morning or dealt with large groups before. We ate in silence, except for when one of us asked for more coffee.

Celicia poured coffee as someone else cleared the table of our plates.

Norm looked up as three men approached. His eyes darted around the diner as if looking for an escape route or an assassin. That concerned me. Before I could react, the three men stood by our booth.

"Long way from L.A., Norm." The man wore a nice suit, clean white shirt and blue tie. Tall and balding, I pinned him as a fed.

"Special Agent in Charge John Parks." Norm forced a cold smile. "Long way from Miami, Agent Parks."

Parks' stare studied us. He frowned and turned to the two men with him. Their stern looks didn't need words.

"You and your friends vacationing?" Norm's icy smile never faltered.

"I got a wake-up call at three this morning." Parks ignored Norm's question, pulled a chair up and sat. "Seems a bunch of pirates attacked a meth lab on the St. Johns River."

"And you drove up here from Miami!" Norm stared at

him. "I hope you caught them."

Parks turned to the two men behind him. "This is Agent John Hubbard, DEA, and Agent Bill Craig, ATF."

Both men dressed in federally approved dark suits. Hubbard stood close to six feet with a wiry frame. Craig, about five-eight and stouter than Parks and Hubbard.

"Gentlemen," Norm turned his attention to those of us at the table. "Agent Parks is with the FBI, in Miami."

"Special Agent in Charge Parks." Parks corrected Norm and I wondered what the hell was going on.

Lawyer Up and Shut Up
Chapter TWENTY-FOUR

"Pauly and I go way back." Hubbard from the DEA stood next to seated FBI Agent Parks. "We've been adversaries for years."

"Adversaries is such a confrontational word." Pauly rubbed his bearded chin as if thinking and smiled at him. "I prefer to think of it as a friendship where friends have different opinions, different takes on things. Like Mick and Norm."

"A couple of bad observations," Parks said. "Norm doesn't have friends or opinions. He gets his orders and obeys them, like a good soldier."

"And the DEA appreciates your work, Norm, don't let Agent Parks discourage you." Hubbard returned Norm's frosty grin.

"They don't let you speak?" After a moment of awkward silence, Norm directed his question to ATF Agent Craig.

Craig nodded toward Pauly, but said nothing. Like me, I guessed, Craig wanted to know where and how Pauly got his hands on such a variety of weapons. Pauly, by his silence, apparently didn't have knowledge of Craig.

"My friends and I've finished breakfast and we're ready to leave. So, what's this is all about?" Norm pushed himself to the edge of the booth.

"We know Mick and Pauly, Norm." Parks ignored Norm's comment. "Are you going to introduce the rest of your gang?"

Norm held Parks' stare and said nothing.

Parks turned to Hubbard and held out his hand. Hubbard took folded papers from inside his suit jacket and handed them over. Parks unfolded the sheets. "I need to talk to you, alone."

"Ain't gonna happen," Norm said.

Parks refolded the papers and drummed them on the table. "I know how you have to operate and you know how I have to."

"Ain't gonna happen, John," Norm said. "Say what you came to say or get out of our way."

Parks looked behind him at Hubbard and Craig. Their expressions stayed blank, leaving the decision in Parks' hands. "It's classified."

Norm began to stand. "Then, if I were you, I wouldn't talk about it in a public restaurant."

"Sit down!" Parks ordered.

"John, I have to wonder how a three-agency operation went ahead without anyone in Homeland Security knowing about it." Norm stared hard at him. "If Homeland knew, JSOC would've at least heard about it and pulled our operation or maybe combined them. Wanna explain that? Can you?"

"Rattlers are not a national security concern," Parks said.

"Since when?" Norm pushed forward.

The rest of us stood up as if on cue.

"Nice talking to you." Norm led the way to the front of the diner, he paid the bill and we left.

I looked behind me as I went through the door and the three agents remained at the booth, their heads bent close together.

Before getting into the Jeep, I said, "What was that about?"

"I bluffed 'em," Norm said. "But if Homeland Security doesn't know what they're up to, it does make me wonder." Opening the door to the Jeep, Norm said, "The undercover agent last night is a fed, one of theirs." Norm got into the Jeep and drove us back to the hotel.

"Which agency?"

"I don't think it matters, Mick." Norm parked the Jeep

behind the hotel to avoid prying eyes from the street. Parks had to know what Norm drove, since he knew where we went for breakfast. "We haven't heard the last from them."

We gathered in Norm's mini-suite for a planning session. "The feds involved is gonna muddy our waters," Norm said to begin. "They probably followed us from the hotel, so avoiding them is a big problem."

"They know your Jeep. What's the chances our vehicles are on their list?" Burt said.

"They'll know who every one of you is, soon enough." Norm looked out the window and then turned back to us. "Stake your life on it. They had someone taking photos of us leaving the hotel this morning or from the restaurant. They'll have dossiers on you and that includes information on any vehicle in your name."

"Me too?" Padre Thomas sounded concerned.

"You might give them a headache, Padre," Norm said. "But if there's anything for them to know, they'll know."

"I'm an Irish citizen," Padre Thomas said, concern still in his voice.

"Legally here?" Norm stared at him as if he knew the answer. "If not, Padre, they'll use that threat of deportation when dealing with you."

Padre Thomas said nothing, as he seemed to melt into the chair he sat in, crunching up, trying to make himself invisible.

"I don't own anything," Pauly said. "That's one of the things Craig loses sleep over. We've crossed paths before."

"Comforting to know, Norm," Texas Rich said. "Will we make the no-fly list?" He almost laughed.

"Do you trust those guys, Norm?" Bob paced the room slowly.

"What do you call trust?"

"This is just a thought." Bob stood still and looked around. "Could you trust them with the info on Morgan?

Would they help us get him, if it meant saving whatever operation they had going? Thinking out loud is all."

"My gut reaction is no, we can't trust them," Norm said. "They ganged up on us, three agencies to deal with the likes of us. No offense meant." Norm grinned. "No one in this room and that includes me, requires that kind of response."

"So why'd we get three of them?" Texas Rich picked the pepperoni off a cold slice of pizza.

"Inter-agency operation." Norm thought aloud. "Not too often that happens. FBI, racketeering, is my guess. DEA, well, we know about the meth labs and the ATF. Gotta be the Rattlers have some heavy hitting power somewhere."

"One biker gang, three agencies to take it down?" Bob shook his head. "I don't see them sharing."

"Me either." Norm checked outside the window again. "That only makes whatever trouble we're causing worse for us."

"You expecting company?" I walked to the window in time to see three carloads of federal agents block the parking lot exits.

"Yeah, without cooperation, they could take us in for obstruction of justice, interfering with a federal investigation." Norm gave a nervous laugh. "If they wanted to, they'd get us for being in Daytona. Everyone knows, right up front, ask for an attorney and then shut up. Got that?"

We all nodded, even Padre Thomas who talked to himself or his angels.

Peripheral guesses
Chapter TWENTY-FIVE

"Everyone ready?" Norm prepared to open the door. *Yeah. Sure. Okay,* responses came from us. He opened the door and stepped outside. Parks came up the stairwell first. I looked out the window toward the other stairway, expecting to see armed federal agents. There were none. Mumbled voices came into the room, but I couldn't make out what they said.

Parks came in first, followed by Craig and Hubbard. No guns, no handcuffs. Uneasy smiles pasted on their faces. Norm closed the door.

The living area of the mini-suite offered inadequate seating and we'd taken it all. I stood by the small kitchen counter. Norm joined me. The agents stood in the room as if on display. I guess they were.

During the silence, eyes darted around, making contact and then moving on.

"Your dime, John." Norm pointed at Parks.

He cleared his throat, looked at the other two agents and lost his nervous grin. "I called Admiral Bolter."

Norm checked his wristwatch. "You get him on the golf course?"

Parks shook his head. "Golf with a congressman is this afternoon." He grinned and tried to sound humorous. He failed.

"His comment about you was the 'I can't comment on an ongoing operation or those involved.' It's classified. Standard press bullshit." Parks took papers from inside his suit coat. "Anyway, I gave him a rundown on our operation. I asked him how we overlapped with whatever your operation is. 'No comment,' he said. 'Ask Norm, it's his operation.' So I'm asking, what are you doing shooting up the Rattlers? What's JSOC got to do with these guys?"

"Don't try saying drugs, Norm," Hubbard said. "They get nothing from Mexico, it's all home cooking and you're not supposed to work this side of the border."

"You have something to say?" Norm turned to Craig.

Craig shook his head.

Norm looked out the window. "Why's the driveway blocked?"

"Don't want to be interrupted," Parks said, trying to put a little humor in his words. He failed again. "If the Rattlers are after you, seeing a federal presence will deter them."

Norm laughed. "Yeah, the only thing it does is convince them we're feds and not drug dealers. Call off the blockade."

"You want them thinking you're drug dealers?" Hubbard said.

"Call it off!" Norm repeated.

Parks nodded and Hubbard used his cell and told the drivers of the vehicles to park.

What I would've given to have been inside Norm's head at that moment. I knew he could think on his feet, on the run, but our situation — my situation, I should say — made it difficult because we'd decided not to ask for their help. Norm didn't trust them. I knew that once the feds' net caught Morgan, state charges, even murder, would be secondary. Norm knew it too.

"Done," Hubbard said.

Norm looked out the window to make sure the vehicles had moved. "I'll make a deal with you," he said.

"We're listening," Parks said.

"Don't interfere with us for four days, no matter what goes down, and then we'll be gone." Norm said with an expression even I couldn't read. "All I can tell you, I can assure you, we are not interested in whatever your operation's goal is."

The three agents laughed, but it sounded more like

nervous than funny laughter.

"Give you free rein for ninety-six hours!" Craig shouted.

"You're fucking nuts."

Parks grabbed onto Craig's arm. "What do we get in return?"

"We go away."

"Leaving us deaf, dumb and blind?" Parks said.

"I'll say it again. What we are doing doesn't affect your operation," Norm said. "If we fail, it won't matter to you, and if we succeed, you'll know what we did but it won't affect your end game with these guys."

"You don't know what we're doing, so how can you say that?" Parks brought it forth as a challenge, to see what Norm knew.

Norm repeated his theory about racketeering, drugs and weapons.

"No more details than that?" Parks said. "All you're telling us is what our agencies do."

"Racketeering is the big net," Norm said. "From stealing motorcycles for parts to money laundering; most any illegal activity, big or small, you can prove against the club will get you the membership. Drugs, the meth labs are no secret, so Hubbard is putting together a Rattlers' distributors list, local suppliers, dealers, especially in this new venture. Some will go to prison, some will become CIs; and Craig wants to know where they're getting the automatic weapons. They aren't too available on the black market, even in Arizona. How am I doing? A bust involving multiple Gulf Coast states would certainly help your careers, boost your status in your agencies."

"Peripheral guesses." Parks still held the folded papers. "Maybe we could help you, if we knew how to."

"You going to smoke those papers, or show me?" Norm reached out expecting the papers.

Parks rolled them into a tube. "These were for you, if you

cooperated." He placed the papers back inside his suit coat. "We have the option of arresting everyone here for a variety of crimes, but I like interfering with a federal investigation best. That should give you your four days in jail."

"And there's the weapons in your cars," Hubbard said. "I bet you pay checks, those four, fully automatic M16s are stolen."

Norm turned to Craig. "Sorry no drugs, unless you can plant them on us."

"Norm, we don't want to do this," Parks said. "Not good inter-agency cooperation."

"And I'd use my one call to reach Admiral Bolter and that would piss him off."

Parks bit his lower lip. Angry, frustrated, maybe beaten at his own game. Whatever it was, he didn't like Norm's threat involving Admiral Bolter. Parks led the two agents outside where they huddled together. Inside we said nothing, keeping our eyes on the three men outside the window.

Forty-eight Hours is All You Have
Chapter TWENTY-SIX

The three agents did a lot of head shaking and finger pointing. Craig and Hubbard turned their backs on Parks, walked away, only to return and shout the word *No* often and loud enough for us to hear in the room with the door closed. Parks finally held his hands up to stop the conflict. Hubbard and Craig looked in agreement as they tried one more argument. Parks shook his head, made a comment and then opened the door. The agents walked in. They weren't smiling.

"The majority decision is to arrest you," Parks said to Norm, upon entering, ignoring the rest of us. "I explained that our agencies are bureaucracies, not democracies, so there's no voting."

"And you called me the good solider, following orders." Norm grinned. "If we're not to be arrested . . ." He left the sentence unfinished.

"We're giving you forty-eight hours to do what it is you have to do. Consider it inter-agency cooperation," Parks said. "But, we're not stepping aside, allowing you free rein. Our agencies will continue their observations, collect what data we can, so we stay on schedule. Understood?"

"You could be in our way." Norm didn't answer the question.

"Since we don't know what you're doing," Parks said, "I can't give you an honest answer."

"I can!" Craig screeched. "If we're in your way, you're affecting our operation and you're in our way! You said you wouldn't do that. So stay the fuck out of our way!"

Parks and Hubbard nodded their agreement.

"Wild guess on my part," Norm said with his devil-may-care grin. "Craig voted for jail."

Parks ignored Norm. "If you affect, or what you are doing threatens, our operation in any way, we'll stop you. Stay outside our circle and do your job in two days."

"And if we can't?" Norm went back to being serious. "Forty-eight hours means we have to rush, push caution aside and that could be messy, if not make this impossible."

"You're breaking my heart, Norm. You've got two choices," Parks said. "Forty-eight hours to do what you need to do, or four days in jail."

"You have a third choice," Hubbard said. "Walk away."

Norm replied with a shake of his head that told the agents, no way.

"Now, before you give me your decision, let me make an assumption." Parks gave a quick scan around. "I think you're telling me the truth and you aren't interested in the Rattlers or anything our agencies are working on." Parks turned to Craig and Hubbard, then back to Norm. "They don't agree with me. I think, in knowing how you've worked in the past, you're after one, maybe two men that are with the Rattlers. The bikers are well armed, you found that out on the river." Parks gave the room another slow once over. "Looking at this group, the bikers would tear you up in a New York minute. So, you're waiting for an opportunity to grab your guy or guys when they're away from the Rattlers or with only a few of them. If it were an assassination, you wouldn't need this company. How am I doing?"

"John, you know I can't comment on an ongoing operation." Norm grinned, quoting Admiral Bolter's statement. We laughed quietly.

"Asshole!" Craig said. "The upside of all this is, if the Rattlers tear you apart, it gives me a reason to go in."

"We don't want anyone being torn up." Parks glared at Craig and that told him to stop. It also showed us who ran the team. "What we want is for you to get done and be gone. We can help, without your violating the need-to-know policy."

"And how's that go?" Norm sounded interested.

"We've got a man inside. You know that," Parks said. "Tell us who you're looking for and maybe he can locate him. Cut most of your work out."

I had the feeling after hearing Craig's outburst that his cooperation would be lacking and he might enjoy our failure enough to initiate it. Norm had been right to avoid their help. It only took one pissed-off agent to make an operation fall apart. The three agents might have been a good team before we arrived, but now they were infighting and that never bodes well for any group.

If they knew about Morgan and helped in capturing him, they'd consider flipping him because it would benefit their task. Norm knew this. Trusting them would have been a mistake and, I realized, would've given support to Morgan's escaping murder charges. He'd cut a deal with them and a federal deal trumps a state charge. Turning on the Rattlers would qualify anyone for federal witness protection.

"I'll ask this," Norm said after a few quiet moments. "Have your man inside do what he can to keep the Rattlers away from us. The rest we can handle on our own."

"That's your best offer?" Hubbard said.

"It's the best I can do, under the circumstances," Norm said.

"If I hear from him within the next forty-eight hours, I'll let him know who and what you are," Parks said. "If I don't hear from him, there's nothing I can do."

"When do the forty-eight hours start?"

"Fifteen minutes ago." Parks opened the door. "Don't call us, we'll call you."

The agents walked out, closed the door and we waited for Norm to say something. He watched out the window as the men walked down to their waiting vehicles. I moved next to him.

"Well?" We turned away from the windows as the cars left the hotel parking lot.

"We aren't in jail." Norm sat at the counter. "They haven't left us much time."

"Why didn't we want their help?" Burt said. "They might have known where Morgan is. Hell, he could be here or anywhere including the Panhandle."

"They know we're looking for someone, but not who," Bob said.

"If they knew who and why, they'd cut us out," I said. "They'd use it to flip Morgan and if he didn't get killed in the crossfire, he'd go into witness protection. We need to get him away from both sides of this battle. He has to pay."

"Forty-eight hours, beginning now, doesn't leave us much time," Bob said. "We can't do anything at the strip club for almost twelve hours."

"Going back to the river is suicide," Burt said.

"We might want to keep an eye on the strip club." Pauly stood up and stretched. "Beats sitting around here and Morgan might come and go at any time. He has to be staying somewhere."

"He wasn't at the fish camp," Norm said. "Cameras haven't picked him up on the road."

"Where do we watch from? The stores on the back street are open," Texas Rich said. "Can't hang around those parking lots too long before someone calls the cops."

"I think Bob and I should take a ride by the Tit-4-Tat and see what goes on there in the day time," Pauly said. "See if we can find a daylight vantage point."

"Like you two did on the river?" Burt said. "I'll go along. Keep you out of trouble."

"We can all go." Norm walked to the door. "We've got time to kill, so might as well see if we have a tail."

"Feds or bikers?" Pauly opened the door and papers that had been stuck in the doorjamb fell.

"Maybe both." Norm stooped and picked up the papers. He unfolded them, glanced at the first page and then walked back into the mini-suite. "Agent Parks' notes."

They're Watching Us
Chapter TWENTY-SEVEN

Norm leaned over and spread the few pages across the kitchenette countertop. He studied them as we looked over his shoulder, knowing better than to ask questions until he finished his evaluation. We could see a list of names, some with thumbnail photos next to them. A couple of pages of what looked like hand-drawn diagrams of floor plans and the last page appeared to be an organizational pyramid.

The pages moved in order as Norm considered their importance. When he stopped shuffling them he stood up straight and stepped back from the counter.

"They give a lot of info." Norm turned to us. "But nothing about Morgan."

"No help, then?" I said, unable to hide my disappointment.

"Help in the fact that we know more about the Rattlers than we did an hour ago," Norm said. "We have their pecking order," Norm returned to the counter and pointed to the command diagram. "We know what some of them look like and a layout of the Tit-4-Tat."

"How does that help?" Texas Rich said.

"We find Morgan and see who's with him. If it's lower level bikers, it's a cakewalk to snatch him," Norm said. "Floor plans don't help us, but we know what's on the second floor now. Maybe Morgan's hiding there."

"The higher up the totem pole a person is, the more guns hanging around, the more difficult to grab Morgan." Pauly had experienced that situation in his old life. "A hierarchy is better protected and it gives us an idea of Morgan's place if he's with them."

"Yeah," Norm said. "Most of these pages are copies of handwritten pieces. Has to be from their inside man . The list," he pointed to the two pages with thumbnail photos, "is typed but some of the names have to come from their man, probably FBI files, too, and then organized into this. So, we don't know how up to date the list is. People like these bikers come and go, usually in a body bag, without obituary notices."

"Who left the pages?" Burt said. "Why not just give them to us?"

"My guess is Parks," Norm said. "We've butted heads before in Mexico City, but he's good. He does what it takes to get the job done."

"So, why leave 'em in the door?" I said.

Norm didn't miss a chance to stick it to Pauly, and he couldn't overlook it now. "Pauly has butted heads, can we say, with Craig and Hubbard. Right?"

Pauly hunched his shoulders. "Never met the men one-on-one," he said. "Heard of them, though."

"And they've heard of your exploits. Some people don't believe in ex-drug smugglers," Norm said, not admitting he was one of those people. "Hubbard and Craig look at Pauly and automatically lump the rest of us in with him. Think of how much help I'd be to the cartel with what I know and what I do. A corrupt military agent. My bet is he's putting money on our wanting to take over the Rattlers' meth operations. Thanks to Pauly being here. Craig and Hubbard don't trust us and don't want to share."

Norm caught me by surprise with his military comment. All the years I've known him, he has denied any connection with the government. He knows I know and I know he knows I know, but we let the lie alone, and don't mention his affiliation with JSOC or the intelligence community, except when arguing.

"Cut to the chase, Norm." You can always count on Bob to do a Joe Friday when the BS is flowing. All he wanted were the facts, not the backstory.

"Might be what Craig said he hopes for." Norm frowned. "We screw up and the bikers tear us a new asshole and that gives ATF reason to get involved. FBI too. Once the meth lab is authenticated the DEA comes in. We could be doing them a favor, dead or alive."

"I'm not in favor of having a second asshole," Bob said and grinned. "What's that leave us?"

"Leaves us where we were before the feds came here," Norm said. "We do surveillance at the Tit-4-Tat, hope for a Hail Mary, and go from there. Excuse the reference, Padre."

Padre Thomas stood quietly off to the side without answering Norm.

"Are we gonna worry about a tail?" Bob said.

Norm looked out the window. "They're watching us. I'd be watching them if situations were reversed. What we've gotta do is keep them unaware of our plans. Snatching Morgan is only half the job now. We've gotta get him back to Key West before they can take him from us."

"You think they'd want him, after we have him?" The thought concerned me.

"If they can put the pieces together of who he is before we get out of here, yes," Norm said. "Who knows what kind of intel they can get out of him. Hell, they might know of the blackmail scheme and want more on the Russians."

"We can't let that happen!" Losing Morgan wasn't an option to me. He had info on Alexei's men in Miami and that could get me closer to Alexei. Two of my worlds collided with Morgan. He had to pay for Robin's death and I needed to kill Alexei.

"When that time comes, Mick, we need to move fast, maybe move Morgan from vehicle to vehicle to confuse the feds as we head south." Again, Norm thought on his feet, putting together a plan before the need arrived.

"If we don't hang around, once we've got him, they might lose interest," Bob said. "He's nowhere on their list."

"My idea exactly," Norm said. "We'll work out a plan to bait and switch the feds when we know how and when we snatch him."

"You're forgetting their inside man knows who we're looking for," Pauly said. "How long before he passes that on or finds Morgan himself?"

"Nothing's going to happen if we sit here." Norm collected the papers, refolded them and put them inside his jacket. "Mick, Padre Thomas and Burt with me. We'll leave now, circle around the streets and drive back on our way to the Tit-4-Tat in about five. Bob, be outside, see if we have a noticeable tail and then follow and meet us on the backstreet of the club. Where we were last night."

"What if they're following me too?" Bob said.

"Nothing we can do about it." Norm opened the door and we got ready to leave. "We try to lose them now, it only brings more attention on us. Until we're ready to make the snatch, let 'em play their games."

"We should be looking for a Rattlers' tail too," Pauly said.

"That goes without saying." Norm led the way out.

The Door Closed Behind Us
Chapter TWENTY-EIGHT

Padre Thomas' abnormal silence began to concern me. No opinions set forth. No whispers to me about what the angels thought.

Norm circled the neighborhood slowly. In less than five minutes, he'd spotted the tail.

"They don't care we know they're there." He laughed.

I adjusted the side mirror and spotted the black SUV. Pauly pulled in a few cars behind the FBI tail as we passed the hotel.

"Original," I said. "Black, with heavy tinted windows all around. Even the windshield. Might as well have FBI stenciled on the side."

"How many of those do you suppose the government has?" Burt turned and waved.

"Hundreds," Norm said. "Why?"

"Volume discounts. Save money for the taxpayers. I wonder how long they keep them?" Burt turned back, maybe disappointed the other driver didn't return his wave.

"Thinking of buying one, Burt?" Norm said.

"Naw. Probably gas hogs." Burt sat back. "Save on the vehicle, pay through the nose for gas. That's the government I know."

When we passed the Tit-4-Tat, two large, bearded bikers stood blocking the driveway with their Hogs. Norm didn't slow down. He took the next left that cut through the neighborhood to the main street behind the strip club.

"If the back parking lot is full, we'll know something's going on." Norm looked for a spot on the street to stop.

"You think it's because of what happened on the river?" I wondered if a meeting concerning the river fiasco would include Morgan.

"By now the bosses over in the Panhandle have considered what happened." Norm parked on the street, in front of an empty storefront. "One of 'em might be here. They could've sent someone to assess the situation."

Across the street, strip mall stores and offices blocked any visual of the Tit-4-Tat's back lot. Pauly found a parking spot a few car lengths up, in front of a neighborhood deli with empty tables on the sidewalk. We met and went into the deli.

With large American coffees, we sat at the outdoor tables. The early afternoon air had a damp chill to it with clouds that did a good job of hiding the sun. Light traffic moved along the street.

From last night's surveillance, we knew that the strip mall had ten shops. Two of them empty, their windows covered with old newspapers; the eight remaining were small shops, an accountant's office and a tax preparer's office. Ann's Seam Shop sat between the two empty shops, blocking street views of the Rattlers' parking lot.

"The feds have to be in one or both of those empty storefronts." Norm sipped his coffee. "Probably on the roof too."

"What's that leave us?" I said.

"Nothing good." Norm stood and looked up and down the street. "If there was only a three-story building on this side, we could use the roof."

"We know they're tailing us." Pauly stood next to Norm. "We know they're across the street. Why hide what we're doing?"

"Meaning?" Norm waited for Pauly's answer.

"Let's walk up the alley and see what there is to see," Pauly said.

"It might just spook the feds," I said. "Seeing us being so obvious. Especially if something's going on."

"It's an option." Norm threw his to-go coffee in the trash; we did the same as we crossed the street.

On the other side of the street, we walked to the east end of the strip mall and turned into the alley.

Norm stopped at the corner of the first building. "Pauly, you stay on the inside and take a good look at the parking lot and whatever else is there. No one else look in that direction."

"Okay." Pauly moved to the building side of the alley.

"Bunch up so he's not in direct line of sight of anyone over there," Norm said.

"Wouldn't people look toward a collection of bikes?" Texas Rich said. "Why aren't we?"

"Yeah, people would, but most people wouldn't be walking down the alley with six friends this late in the afternoon." Norm began to walk. "Unless they were up to no good."

"Do you think they'll stop us?" I walked alongside Norm, seeing the parking lot full of motorcycles in my peripheral vision.

"Who?" Norm looked straight ahead but I knew he scanned the parking lot.

"The FBI?"

"We'll know soon enough." Norm kept walking.

Nervous small talk filled the short distance and then we were next to the empty stores. Ann's backdoor stood open. Norm looked in. A woman sat at a table with a soda and sandwich. She waved and Norm returned it.

We'd gone a few steps further when we heard the door for one of the empty shops behind us open. We stopped.

"Get in here!" FBI Special Agent in Charge John Parks' voice ordered from the darkness.

We followed Norm into the murky room. The door closed behind us.

The Dark Became a Ghostly Grey
Chapter TWENTY-NINE

After coming into the room from the sunny street, my eyes took a while to adjust to the darkness. From across the room, computer screens flickered like one-eyed predators in the night. Still and video cameras perched on tripods appeared as lonely stick-figure soldiers on guard duty, by the newspaper-covered windows. Outside the windows, the back lot of the Tit-4-Tat sat full of motorcycles that we were able to see through tears in the papers. Hushed voices that whispered in the dark became silent as the door closed behind us.

As my eyes adjusted, the dark became a ghostly grey. Small wattage bulbs dotted the room like giant fireflies; dim lamplight circled each computer and desk. Not counting us, there were six other shadowy figures in the room.

"What the hell were you doing, Norm?" Parks' voice overpowered the stillness of the surroundings. He stood in the middle of the room, by the computer printer, more of a shadow figure than a man.

"The bikers have the parking lot blocked off out front." Norm kept his voice low. "We wondered why?"

Parks shook his head. "Why not just walk up and ask them?"

"That's plan C," Norm said.

"What's plan B?"

"Coming in here."

"You should've tried next door." Parks ignored Norm's quip. "Craig and Hubbard would welcome your help!" Parks' satirical comments were better than his attempts to be humorous.

"What can you tell us about the gathering outside?" Bob broke into the conversation.

"Can we look at the photos and videos of who's coming

and going?" Norm said.

"I can tell you nothing and no, you can't view the photos and video." Parks' voice returned to normal.

Norm laughed, turned to us and shook his head. "We might as well keep to our schedule." Norm began to walk away.

"What's your schedule? Plan A?" Parks said.

"Need-to-know." Norm kept walking toward the back door.

"Maybe you can tell me who you're looking for and I can check what we have." Parks' words stopped Norm. "You can't just go through FBI files, Norm. You know that."

"We're looking for a big guy, without the beard." Norm turned and walked back toward Parks. "He'd be with one or two others, maybe even someone from the Panhandle."

"Got a name?"

"Yeah."

Parks waited a beat. "I'm willing to share information with you, the least you can do is tell me who I'm looking for."

"It's a need-to-know situation," Norm repeated. "According to Admiral Bolter, the FBI isn't on the need-to-know list."

"A lot of people have come and gone." Parks pointed toward the newspaper-covered window. "I've got ID on most of them."

"Not on this one," Norm said. "John, let's cut the bullshit, okay? Ninety-nine percent of those bikers dress and look alike. Ratty hair, ratty beard, beer belly and draped in grimy denim. My man would stand out like J. Edgar in a dress at an FBI dance."

Parks walked to a computer desk and opened a large manila envelope. I wondered if he or any FBI agents took offense at Norm's joke about J. Edgar Hoover.

My eyes had adjusted and I could make out that Parks

took papers from the envelope. The other agents in the room went about whatever their duties were without interfering with us, voices muted.

Parks walked to Norm and handed him three eight-by-ten photos. "One of these him?"

Norm studied the photos. I'm not sure why. He'd never met Morgan and all he knew is that Morgan's big as a horse and dumb as a goldfish.

Norm handed me the photos. I couldn't see clearly, so I went to a computer desk and looked at the photos under the light. The photos, copied onto cheap photo paper, had a sharpness that impressed me. Two of the photos showed men with short beards and hair. The third photo showed Morgan in his Rattler denim outfit, with stubble on his chin, no beard. Whoever printed the photo had cropped out people around Morgan. I handed two photos to Norm and shook my head.

"It's him." I held the photo of Morgan. On the back, a small form taped to it had information. Name, *unknown*, it read and then gave today's date. For time it read *12:33 PM.*, followed by location.

Norm took it from me.

"He's inside?" Norm gave Parks the photos back.

"Only a handful have left." Parks took the photos. "But if this is the guy, he hasn't."

Norm nodded. "How many do you think are inside?"

Parks walked us to the window and peeked through a hole in the paper that the camera used to shoot through.

"I'd say about fifty bikes." Parks pulled back and let Norm have a look. "One to a bike, they left their old ladies home. What's going on in there is business."

"About fifty," Norm said after looking.

"The club opens in less than an hour," Parks said.

"Your guy inside?" Norm stood up.

Parks nodded. "Did you look at the floor plan?" He had

left the papers at the hotel door for us.

"Skimmed them. Not too interested in going in there," Norm said. "Wait for him to leave is the best plan."

"There's a meeting room on the second floor," Parks said. "Like a corporation board room, with the large conference table and all."

"What else is there?" Norm said.

"Two small rooms with cots," Parks said. "And one small room used as a holding cell."

"Anyone in it?"

"Won't know till later," Parks said. "You can observe from here, if you don't get in the way of our work."

"What's your work?" Norm was leery of the offer.

"Photos. See who's there. See who's new to the club and who's who. We aren't trying to snatch anyone, just observe."

"What about them?" Norm pointed toward the other vacant shop.

"Much the same." Parks remained elusive in regards to the DEA and ATF. "If they find someone that's wanted, they have men prepared to stop and arrest the person on the streets."

"You haven't bugged the place?" Bob said.

"Downstairs it's too noisy when they're hanging around and the dancers are on stage." Parks' sudden cooperation baffled me. "Upstairs, they actually scan for bugs every day. They're not all assholes."

"Ex-military," Burt said.

"Yeah, ex-military that hasn't forgotten all that Uncle Sam taught 'em," Parks said. "I've been on these guys for a couple of years and I have to keep reminding myself this isn't a military operation."

"That's a mistake on your part," Norm said. "They think and act military. They train their foot soldiers to respond like soldiers. Craig seems to think they have military weaponry. The rifles we took from them were automatics, not store-bought semis."

Parks didn't comment. He walked across the room, briefly talked to a couple of his agents and then came back to us, the two in tow. We didn't talk. We kept watch on Parks.

"Make yourselves at home," Parks said. "We've ordered pizza. Sorry, no beer."

"We have what we need," Norm said. "Our man's inside. We can stakeout across from the club's entrance and catch him when he leaves."

"But can you have pizza and keep out of the cold?" Parks grinned and it was visible even in the grayness.

"You want something." Norm cut his sentence short. "No, you need something from us."

Still grinning Parks nodded his head. "Let's discuss it over pizza."

Say Gitmo *and the FBI Steps Back*
Chapter THIRTY

FBI Special Agent in Charge John Parks looked nervous as a vampire at sunrise while he waited for Norm to respond. Norm said I had to come along. Parks said no. Norm said no thanks then. Parks nodded his halfhearted okay and walked us to a windowless closet-size room that held a couch. A sixty-watt bulb hung from above. Parks closed the door. Norm and I sat. Parks stood.

He looked at me and I could see he didn't like an outsider being involved. Big problem with the feds is they've lost any connection to the public and live within a sphere that isolates them. We're not all bad guys, but that's the way they treat the public. Often times, I've felt the feds make Jack Webb's Joe Friday seem fuzzy and warm.

Something had screwed up and if Norm could fix it, it only meant violence and death. It also meant the feds wanted to distance themselves from it. What I thought was my well-crafted plan to snatch Morgan and head back to Key West lost its simplicity on the Saint Johns River. I had a feeling it was about to morph into disaster.

"What do you need?" Norm said after a few awkward moments of silence.

Parks hesitated. "I might not need anything."

"But you're not sure."

Parks nodded. "My man inside hasn't made contact since last night."

"After the river fiasco they could be scrambling."

"I thought of that, Norm." Parks leaned against the flimsy wall then pushed away as he realized it wouldn't support him. "He didn't have to call in. We have small signals. He switches his wristwatch to his right wrist if he needs out. Riding the bike, scarf inside the jacket, all is okay. Outside the jacket, he's in trouble. His jacket on a peg outside the meth lab. Lot of those things."

"I'm familiar with their use," Norm said.

"He wasn't one of the bikers coming in this morning. All those bikes out there, none of them are his."

"He stayed at the river," Norm said. "They wouldn't abandon the meth lab."

"We have spotters there. Nothing. People there, yes. No sign of our man."

"If you're that concerned, go in, make your bust now," Norm said.

"We're this close." Parks held up his hand, the thumb and forefinger almost touching. "We're talking about making hundreds of arrests. Our nets are going to catch the minnows and whales of this gang. I can't throw it all away because I have a bad feeling in my gut."

"Something else?"

Parks hesitated. "Early this morning the night crew reported a van pulled up and four people hustled a fifth inside. A boss from the Panhandle or maybe a prisoner for their holding cell."

"Gut telling you it's the latter?"

Parks nodded as he ran his hand across his mouth. He knew his telling us this wouldn't meet with approval from higher ups.

"We grab Morgan and make him tell us about your man," I said. "Then we know for sure."

Parks looked at me. "Morgan? That's who you're after, a guy named Morgan?"

"Good work, hoss." Norm looked at me as you'd look at a misbehaving child. "Yeah, Morgan Pryce. From here he's on his way to Gitmo."

"A terrorist?" Parks seemed surprised. "With the Rattlers?"

"Home-grown terrorist." Norm lied. "Worst kind. We

need to find out why he's connecting with the Rattlers. And with Russian gangsters. It will be easier to do it at Gitmo. You understand why it's not for distribution to other agencies."

Norm thinking on his feet, again. Damn, he's good, I thought. That scenario came out of nowhere. Say *Gitmo* and even the FBI steps back.

Parks locked his fingers together and cracked his knuckles. "Can you imagine the damage these bikers could do throughout the South? Bridges, railroads, nothing would be safe."

"Yeah, but that's my problem, John," Norm said. "What about your problem?"

"I can't go in there without a warrant," Parks finally said. "I'm spread thin here anyway. My guys walk in there naked, they'd still look like FBI agents."

"You wear a uniform, just like the Rattlers. Cleaner, different, but still a uniform," Norm said.

"Yeah and it usually works for us," Parks said. "I need you to visit the strip club when it opens and see if our man is visible."

Park's nervous expression told me this wasn't a sanctioned request.

"If he isn't?" Norm said.

"There's a few discrete signs you can leave for him," Parks said. "A word printed on the men's room wall, a colored ribbon placed under the bar top. Things like that. He'll know to make contact right away, if he's able."

"In and out. Easy as that?" Norm didn't sound convinced.

"Enjoy the naked women, have a beer or two. Piss in the john and leave," Parks said. "Maybe take him with you. Two tourists. Two guys on the town."

"Morgan knows me, I can't go in." I said.

"Norm can go by himself, or take one of your other pals," Parks said.

"Pauly, Bob, Norm and I, we've been seen at the river site," I said.

"Only seen by your man and one other biker," Norm said. "I could go in with Burt or Texas Rich."

"Norm, going in there is like plan Z on our list," I said. "Even you can't take on fifty bikers."

"You can't go in armed, either," Parks said. "They see a weapon and you're fucked."

"There's no way this spells anything but disaster," I said, almost stammering.

"It's an FBI problem." Norm looked at Parks. "Bust them now, get your man out and give us Morgan."

"It's not a decision I can make," Parks said. "They'd never go for it." He pointed to the next empty building that held the DEA and ATF agents. He cared about the man while others put the assignment first.

"I can go in alone," Norm said. "Two beers and I'm out of there."

"What if your man isn't there?" I wondered how far ahead Parks had planned. "What if he's upstairs?"

"Then we might have to go in," Parks said.

"Tell me the codes he'll understand," Norm said. "I'll go in about ten."

It Gets More Complicated
Chapter THIRTY-ONE

I have gut feelings too, and they were doing backflips in my stomach as the conversation ended.

"Hold on, Norm!" I almost shouted as I got up from the couch, but stopped myself in time. I couldn't keep my anger hidden. "Morgan's my problem. We agreed on following a plan, not this. I have a say on what we're doing and I say no!" Norm's expression was ambiguous as my frustration grew. "They're my friends and no one signed on for what you're planning."

Parks looked hard at me, confused at first and then uncertain. He turned his gaze to Norm, waiting for an explanation.

"A long story, John." Norm stood. "You got the synopsis."

We were in each other's space as we argued in the small room.

"I wonder." Parks' look didn't soften as his concern for who and what we were grew. "Are you in or not?"

Norm scratched the back of his neck with his left hand and I saw the grimace of pain on his face from the bullet wound to his arm yesterday at the river.

"Mick, one of our own's life is at stake. What if it was you?" Norm spoke softly, bringing his left arm to his side. His words carried determination. He planned to go it alone if neccssary. I knew the tone. "Right now it has nothing to do with Morgan. He might be an extra bonus for us, or he might not."

"What about the rest of us? You're putting our lives in danger," I said.

"I'm not asking anyone to come with me," Norm said. "My plan is simple, go in, have a beer or two and leave the codes so the agent contacts John."

I turned to Parks. "You think it's gonna be that simple after what happened on the river? You think that gathering out there is a celebration? More likely, it's a war council."

"Simplicity is what I hope for." Parks turned toward me, his look remained hard. He hadn't swallowed Norm's story about terrorists and Gitmo.

"You're bullshitting each other and I'm not buying it." This time my voice came out loud. "Why'd you leave floor plans for us? You wanted Norm to know the layout." I spoke to Parks.

He looked at Norm.

I turned to Norm. "You have to go upstairs! If he's been found out, you have to."

"Not if I see him downstairs."

Norm came looking for Morgan to help me. He knew I wouldn't let him go alone. My argument had been lost before it started.

"Where are the floor plans?" I said.

We followed Parks out of the room to a large table by the street entrance to the shop.

Most everyone stood around eating pizza, including Bob, Pauly, Burt, Texas Rich and Padre Thomas. They ignored us so purposely I knew my voice had carried outside the small room.

Parks unfolded blue prints of the Tit-4-Tat. "First floor, street and parking. In front, a small security office, hallway leading to the main room." He pulled out the bottom sheet. "Upstairs. This is the stairway up and it's accessible only from the back. One-way up. One-way down." Then he pointed to the back double door on the first page and moved his finger to the markings for a stairway. "Hold on." Parks went to the pizza table and pulled a man away. They walked to us.

Bob and Pauly looked toward us but stayed put.

"This is Agent Steve Turtell." Parks introduced him to Norm. "He's one of our marksmen. Steve has two purposes on the river. With his scope, he can stay back out of sight and still watch the meth operation and look for our man's signals. If necessary, he's in a good position to help our man run, if called for."

"Why are *we* meeting Agent Turtell?" I didn't like Parks ignoring me.

Again, the hard look before Parks spoke. "There are two sentries on the back door and the two bikers blocking the driveway. Agent Turtell will take them out prior to your going in."

"Hold on J. Edgar, why would Norm need anyone taken out, if he's only going in to check for your agent or leave a sign?" I raised my palms. Norm grinned. "You never planned this to be an in-and-out operation for one man!"

Norm grabbed my arm. "Mick, you need to quiet down." He put pressure on my arm and kept his voice above a whisper. "This is what I do. I didn't create the situation, but maybe I can help. I could use your help. And theirs." He nodded toward the pizza table.

I turned to Parks and Turtell. "If this is so important, and your man's life is in danger, why not use the FBI SWAT team? Even the local police? You're involving civilians."

Norm let go of my arm.

"It gets more complicated," Parks said.

"How the hell is that possible?" I looked at Norm because I felt he knew what was going on. Parks would lie. Maybe Norm wouldn't.

"You can't get caught." Parks and Turtell nodded in agreement. "The FBI will not support any claims you make indicating we're involved."

"I see no problem in that." My sarcasm didn't go over well. "That's why we carry a cyanide capsule." I pushed Norm and stood back from him. "You want to go in there, against fifty deranged bikers who are probably armed to the teeth with automatic weapons, looking for someone we aren't even sure is there? Am I missing something?"

"Yeah," Norm said. "If we're caught, we're fucked!"

"Mick, Take the Twelve Gauge"
Chapter THIRTY-TWO

My gut still did backflips, but now my head spun like a carrousel out of control. No matter how I looked at the situation, there was no way we could go up against fifty better-armed bikers, on their turf, and walk away breathing. It called for the SWAT team, but Special Agent in Charge Parks wouldn't, or couldn't call them in. And Norm went along with the decision.

Someone yelled Parks' name from the back of the room. We all turned as he hurried away. I looked at Norm. His expression remained as cold as granite.

I went to follow Parks and Norm grabbed my arm.

"You need to trust me, Mick."

I glanced toward my friends, there to help me, not die for me. "I can't, Norm." I pulled away.

Parks and a few other agents stood in front of a computer monitor watching a video of the Tit-4-Tat parking lot, taken from a camera poking through a hole in the paper that covered the back window. No sound came from the monitor, but loud throttling Harley engine noise pushed into the darkened room from outside.

"Any chance you saw him?" Norm said.

Parks shook his head. "We'll go back and look at the feed when they're gone. Run it slow motion."

"Caught us by surprise," Turtell said.

"Morgan? Are you looking for Morgan?" I said.

Parks turned to me. "When we go through the feed you can look for him."

As the engine noise faded, and most turned away from the monitor, Parks' phone rang. He answered it, keeping a distance from us.

"How many bikers drove off?" Norm asked Turtell.

"Most of them. Ten, maybe twelve bikes left in the lot," Turtell said. "Meeting's over, I guess." He turned to where Parks stood in the shadows, talking on his phone. "Could be bad news, them leaving in mass. When the Rattlers sentence you, there's no appeal."

"You're thinking worse case," Norm said. "They wouldn't kill him there."

"Tape a plastic bag over his head," Turtell said. "Take the body out with the trash."

Bob and Pauly walked next to me. I tapped Norm's shoulder and he followed us back to the table with the blueprints.

"You should buy a lotto ticket, Norm." I spoke softly as we walked.

"Why's that, hoss?"

"You're having a run of luck." I knew that our chances of going into the Tit-4-Tat and walking out alive, with or without the men we were looking for, had improved tenfold with most of the Rattlers leaving.

Using the blueprints, Norm explained to the others what he had in mind for entering the strip club looking for the undercover agent and Morgan, but left no doubt the agent took priority. Bob and I would go in the front. Our job was to disable the two security bikers at the entrance. Norm, Pauly, Texas Rich and Burt would go in through the back. Norm and Burt to rush upstairs to check the holding cell for the agent. Pauly and Texas Rich downstairs. The idea being that our attack from the front and the back of the club would confuse the bikers and give Norm the few minutes he needed upstairs.

Norm introduced Agent Turtell and the agent assured us he would take out the club's exterior security and be there to cover our retreat.

When Turtell had finished explaining how he'd support our exit, Parks joined us.

"Once the shooting starts, you've got three, maybe four minutes to get out," Parks said. "We've got your back, so head this way and your cars will be waiting on you."

"You have to take care of Padre Thomas," I said. "Someone needs to get him back to the motel before all this goes down."

"Not a problem," Parks said. "Anything else?"

"Yeah," Bob said. "I need a suppressor for a Kimber."

Parks gave Norm one of his looks.

"If I have to shoot the security guys, our surprise is over," Bob said. "That's taking thirty-seconds or more off whatever time we have inside and our surprise is blown."

I think Bob made shooting the security guys a last option because Padre Thomas stood close by. We all knew what he had to do. No doubt, Padre Thomas did too.

"We've got an hour before we go in." Norm looked at his wristwatch. It was ten-thirty. "Can you get one?"

"If we can't, we'll make one from a plastic soda bottle," Parks said.

"Good for only one shot," Bob said. "I'm gonna need two shots."

Parks looked at me as the second shooter. Norm shook his head. He couldn't count on me for that.

"Let me work on it." Parks took his phone from his jacket and left us.

"You have to leave, Padre." It concerned me that, since we'd been inside, Padre Thomas had remained quiet. "We'll pick you up when this is all over."

"Yes, I understand." He went to the table with the large coffee urn.

"Mick, take the twelve gauge," Pauly said. "And the dragon's breath shells. I'll do the same. A couple of those shots will confuse them."

"What about the girls and whoever's come in to see them?" Burt said. "There could be innocent customers in there. And maybe they're drunk. Not a good mixture for what we're doing."

"As long as we have surprise going, we should be okay," Norm said. "By the time the bikers start shooting back, the girls will be gone and the customers will be on the floor."

"What if they run?" Burt said.

"Yell at them to get down, demand it and most will be panicked and obey." Norm looked toward Parks. "Bob, can you use something besides the Kimber?"

"I guess so," Bob said. "As long as it has a suppressor."

"I left everything but my handgun in the truck," Burt said. "I should drive back with Padre Thomas and get the truck."

"No time." Norm checked his wristwatch again. "Less than an hour."

When I looked around the dim room, I couldn't see Padre Thomas.

We walked outside, checked on the Jeeps, got the duffel bags and went back inside without conversation.

Parks and Turtell joined us as we went through the duffel bags Pauly had supplied.

"Anything happening?" Norm checked his M4 and a dozen thirty-round magazines.

"Not for the bikers," Parks said. "There are ten or twelve civilians in there."

"How many dancers?" Norm put a magazine into his M4.

"Two stages, a dancer on each stage, and there are usually six girls working the tables. DJ in back somewhere, playing music." Parks looked at Turtell who nodded his agreement.

"We could use vests and a few flash-bang grenades," Norm said. "Any chance?"

"Vests aren't a problem." Parks looked at his wristwatch. "Suppressor is on its way. I don't know if we have time to add the grenades."

"Whatever you can do." Norm's quiet tone of voice had a hard edge to it.

Turtell came back carrying the bulletproof vests and handed them out, suggesting they go under the shirt. We all knew that. Turtell had the sizes right and that should have set off my curiosity. That would've led to questions. Later, when I remembered the vests and not asking questions, it had become too late to matter.

The vests fit comfortably.

Pauly made a joke about how thin it was and Norm and Turtell spoke up, assuring us it would stop a forty-five slug.

"Hurt like hell." Norm laughed softly. "Maybe knock you down, but it won't penetrate the vest."

"You have three to four minutes after the first shots are fired, to get in and out," Parks said. "Try not to get yourself shot and you won't have to find out how well the vest works."

Finally, something we all agreed on.

Most dropped to the floor, crying
Chapter THIRTY-THREE

At eleven-fifteen, an agent drove Bob and me to the Tit-4-Tat and parked in the shadows across the street. We sat waiting. I had the bandolier of dragon-breath shotgun shells across my chest. My loaded Sig sat in its concealed holster in my back and I had six, fifteen-round magazines in my jeans' and jacket pockets. All the extra weight slowed me down. One of Norm's axioms on ammunition, *Too much or too little for what's to come.*

Bob got his suppressor, but Parks didn't come up with the flash-bang grenades.

The darkness kept us from seeing clearly down the driveway. Two guards still blocked off the back parking lot, even though most of the Rattlers had left.

If Turtell shot as well and quickly as he said, our sign to enter the front of the club would be when the two bikers went down. The plan called for Turtell to neutralize the two sentries at the back entrance first.

"Seems crazy," Bob whispered.

"Yeah. Morgan coming here, the feds being here. Why are we doing their job?"

"I'm surprised Pauly's gone along this far."

"I guess we're on the path to hell he worried about," I said.

"The river was the gates to hell, Mick." Bob's words came out hard. "When that biker came back, he didn't have our wallets, but I know he had orders to kill us. Now, we could be walking into the fire pits of hell in a few minutes. Something's off-kilter with this whole thing."

Bob surprised me. "Why didn't you say something earlier in there?" I pointed down the driveway toward the federal agents' location.

"What? Padre Thomas gonna take my place?" His tone lightened. "I had doubts, but when the bikers began to leave, the odds kind of fell to our favor."

I checked my wristwatch. "Eleven-thirty."

Even the agent in the front seat stared toward the two bikers in the driveway. I watched one sentry go down as his head exploded like a melon. The other man crouched, looked around, searching for the shooter. His hand held a semi-automatic handgun, twisting, looking for something to shoot at. He stood, pushed himself against the building. Turtell's shot spread most of his skull and brain against the club's wall as his body slid to a sitting position. The darkness of the driveway covered up the grisly carnage.

Head shots from the distance where Turtell hid impressed me and at night, too. He lived up to his own bravado.

Without a word, Bob opened the door and we got out. The car pulled away. We rushed to the club's front door. Six cars took up the parking spots under the Tit-4-Tat sign.

Bob signaled me to open the door. I opened it. Bob rushed in, his Kimber pointed straight out. I walked in, the shotgun leading the way. Two soft pops. Bob removed the suppressor. I looked to my right into the small room and two bikers lay dead on the floor, shot in the chest. Blood puddled around the bodies.

No gunshots came from the main room. Loud rock 'n' roll music almost washed out the wolf whistles and yells from the patrons. We leaned against the hallway wall, just before the main room. I kept the shotgun to my side, but the bandolier remained visible. Across from us, Pauly and Texas Rich stood by what must have been the stairway to upstairs. They waited for Norm to begin shooting or walk back down.

"Big round table up by the stage, to your left," Bob said. "Shoot there."

"Bikers, right?" I had to be sure.

"Six of 'em, ugly as sin."

Getting half of what we'd expected to be ten or twelve Rattlers seemed like good luck. "Do you see Morgan?"

Bob shook his head as he eyed what he could of the room. I wondered if we'd even hear shots from the second floor because of the thunderous music and chatter.

We didn't need to hear. Pauly and Texas Rich walked away from the stairway toward the club's main room. Pauly leading with the shotgun. Texas Rich holding his .357.

"Step out, look left and shoot at the table," Bob said. "Don't hesitate. I've got your back."

We stepped into the main room. Everyone's attention seemed focused on the two stages with a naked woman on each, gyrating to the beat of the music. The crowd of men whistling and shouting.

I looked left, saw the table of six bikers, aimed high to avoid tables close by and fired. With so few patrons and bikers, the large room looked empty, another piece of good luck for us.

Dragon's Breath shells are primarily magnesium pellet shards. It's deadly and the visual effect it produces is impressive, similar to a short-ranged flamethrower.

The shell exploded from my shotgun, sending a corridor of fire forward to hit the bikers behind the neck and head and set them on fire. The two with their backs to me exploded into flames, the other four smoldered from their greasy hair. All jumped up. The tables, chairs, and floor in the path caught fire. I shot again, higher and the ceiling caught on fire.

Pauly fired toward the other stage. He shot three times, brightening the room with flickering flame. I fought the desire to turn and look. Instead, I fired one more shot at the standing, panicking bikers as they began to scatter.

Screams filled the room as heat and smoke from the flames grew. The three shots from me and the three from Pauly covered the room with a deafening noise, fire and a scorching stench. Burning flesh is potent and overpowering. Shouts echoed from one side of the room to the other. Most patrons dropped to the floor, crying and praying aloud.

Two bikers grabbed men off the floor and used them as shields as they backed up toward the stage exit. Firing wildly in my direction as they moved. Texas Rich shot one in the knee and as he slumped, the second shot of the .357 tore his right arm apart, splattering blood and bone onto the hostage as he screamed and fell to the floor. The other biker hugged his hostage tighter and disappeared through the stage's exit.

Bob shot two of the bikers that were still smoldering. Parts of the club began burning fiercely, sending dark smoke across the ceiling.

The four of us scanned the burning room, as flames lapped up the walls. No bikers returned fire. Our element of surprise and the bikers' lack of preparedness had worked for us.

Bob said something but his muffled words didn't make sense to me. My ears rang from the few minutes of gunfire. He pointed across the room and Pauly signaled us to come. Using his shotgun, Pauly indicated upstairs.

As Bob and I walked across the room, a few panicked civilians made a wild dash toward the front exit. Others followed. No one looked at us as we crossed, pushing turned-over tables and chairs out of our way.

Bob shot twice as bikers stood, guns in hand. Bob was quicker. Texas Rich kept watch as we made our way to him.

"Lot of shooting upstairs." Pauly walked toward the stairway. "I think Norm could use some help."

My ears still rang and my hearing remained muffled, but I heard Pauly. I couldn't hear shooting from upstairs.

Pauly wanted me to go upstairs with him, leaving Bob and Texas Rich to cover us in case Rattler reinforcements from Daytona Beach rushed in.

"Our four minutes are almost gone," Bob said loud

enough for me to hear.

"Does anyone hear sirens?" I asked as the shrieking from the main room dwindled. Most of the civilians had made it outside. Cell phones must have been busy calling 911. Maybe none of us would hear sirens until we saw flashing lights and then we would be in deep shit.

No one answered me.

Pauly tapped my arm with his shotgun. "Add shells." He loaded more shells into the shotgun.

I added three, replacing the ones I'd shot. We headed upstairs.

He Smiled and Kept Shooting
Chapter THIRTY-FOUR

Pauly and I hugged opposite walls as we made our way up the stairwell. Even with my clogged ears, I could hear the shooting as we neared the top step. Rapid fire, without stopping I was unable to distinguish the reports of Norm's or Burt's M4s from whatever the Rattlers were shooting. From the hurried, multiple gunshots, I knew the Rattlers outgunned them and wondered why they hadn't retreated.

Bullets tore into the wall above us, shattering the old wood paneling and pockmarking the ceiling. The stench of burnt gunpowder became overpowering as we neared the landing. Heat from the fire below pressed against my back. Dressed for the cold outside, I began perspiring, rivulets of sweat running down my arms and legs.

We squatted and inched our way up the final steps, the shotguns in front. We couldn't shoot until we knew where Norm and Burt were, especially with Dragon's Breath shells. Fire didn't discriminate.

The wide second-floor hallway ran most of the building's length. I spotted Burt off to the right, shooting from a doorway. Pauly mouthed *Norm* and pointed to my left. I nodded my understanding and indicated Burt off to the right. We backed down two steps to avoid being in the line of fire.

"We've gotta stand to shoot." Pauly looked agitated. "Otherwise we'll get Norm and Burt, too."

He hadn't signed on for this. Just the opposite.

"You cover me with your Glock. Gives me time to stand, Pauly. A third shooter might confuse them and all I need is one shot." I had told Pauly this wouldn't happen, before we left Key West. "That should cover us getting the hell downstairs."

"Maybe I should call a cease-fire and when they stop

shooting we'll both stand up," Pauly answered sarcastically.

"Got a better idea?"

Pauly looked at his wristwatch. "Don't have time for a better idea. See if we can get either Norm or Burt's attention. They lay down rapid fire, we stand, shoot and duck!"

"How much time do we have?"

"About thirty seconds. Bob or Texas Rich will let us know when they hear sirens." Without waiting, Pauly began moving toward the landing.

I followed, still bent over and hugging the left wall.

Two blasts with Dragon's Breath shells would set fire to everything in the hall. I assumed the Rattlers were shooting from side room doorways, like Norm and Burt. I had no idea how many there were, but from the heavy shooting, it sounded like it could be as many as six. If only a couple of them were able to avoid the blasts of magnesium pellets and get back into the room, the fire would miss them. Until it began to spread. They'd be trapped and eventually burn to death. I had a feeling they'd come out shooting first. A bullet is quicker and less painful than fire.

If it all went as planned, the fire and smoke would protect us for the few seconds we needed to escape down the stairs and out the back with Norm and Burt.

What if Norm wanted to find the holding cell and the undercover agent? The last thing Norm ever wanted to do was leave a man behind, alive or dead. I learned that about him long ago.

Pauly made all kinds of hand signals in Norm's direction and then I saw Burt glance our way. He smiled as he kept shooting. A half dozen magazines scattered on the floor. He couldn't have many left.

"On the count of three." Pauly looked at me to be sure I understood.

I mouthed *three*.

Pauly held his left hand high enough for Norm to see. One

finger. Two fingers. Three fingers. Norm and Burt moved out of the protective doorways, crouched and laid down rapid fire toward the Rattlers.

Pauly and I stood, took the last step to the landing and fired. Norm and Burt dropped to the floor to avoid any spray of magnesium. Flames instantly engulfed the hallway. The ceiling and walls crackling as fists of fire spread. The Rattlers' shooting stopped as soon as the first flames came from our shotguns. We shot two more times and bent down. Walls, flooring and ceiling ignited along the hallway. The flashes of fire from the Dragon's Breath shells, bright and hot, exploding, turned the whole area into a turbulent firestorm.

Norm and Burt stood, but instead of coming to us, they moved two doors down. Burt kept watch, inches from the flames. Norm shot the lock. He kicked in the door. Fire slicing at its edges. Smoke began to fill the burning hallway. Breathing became labored. Hot as the gates to hell. I half expected the old Greek god Hades to walk out of the fire with the goddess Persephone. We had fallen victim to Mick Murphy's Law.

Shots came from down the fire-engulfed hall. Pauly yelped. Fell down to the smoldering floor. I ran to him. He held his stomach. Burt shot into the wall of fire and smoke.

"Fuck! It hurts." Pauly's vest had stopped the bullet but his body had absorbed the impact force from the shot.

I helped him up. The crackling noise of the fire continued to spread toward us, pushing black smoke and heat. More wild shots came in our direction.

Norm rushed out of the room carrying a man over his shoulder, firefighter style. Burt let Norm pass and then kept shooting into the fire as he backed up. Random shots continued, followed by dark, thick smoke.

Bob came up the stairs and when Norm waved him off, he helped me with Pauly.

"Sirens," he said.

Smoke and flames filled the club's first floor. The heat was unbearable and breathing remained difficult as we hurried out the back door. Cold, fresh air greeted us. The two Rattler sentries lay sprawled between their motorcycles, victims of Turtell's accuracy. No action came from the FBI stakeout location, as we sprinted through the parking lot.

"Where's our help?" I yelled between chilly breaths.

Pauly moved on his own. The grimace on his face said he still had pain.

Texas Rich ran ahead. Norm carried the injured agent. Burt continued to cover our backs.

A motorcycle engine revved. We twisted our heads, looking for the source. With lights off, the motorcycle moved quickly from the shadows of the back fence toward us. Two men on it. One shooting. Texas Rich shot back, then stopped. The bike's passenger shot him from a few yards away. Texas Rich fell. The bike sped past. The passenger shooting wildly at us, as the motorcycle rushed to escape the sirens' arrival.

"Where the hell's Turtell?" I ran to Texas Rich.

Burt came up next to me. We both lifted him to his feet. Once again, the bulletproof vest stopped the bullet but not the impact effect. One shot tore into Texas Rich's shoulder. Blood seeped down his jacket's sleeve.

Between Burt and me, and with a little of his own power, Texas Rich limped to the fence. Federal agents rushed out the back of their building, helped Norm with the undercover agent and then assisted Pauly over the fence. Norm helped us with Texas Rich.

The fire lit up the night, sending moving shadows through the parking area. Smoke rose above the two-story building as flames shot out the second-story windows.

As we closed the door to the surveillance room, flashing lights filled the street in front of the burning Tit-4-Tat.

"Morgan drove, that's why I stopped shooting." Texas Rich moaned as an agent removed his jacket, tore his shirtsleeve and tended to the wound.

"Morgan?" I shouted.

Texas Rich nodded.

"Where the hell's Parks?" I looked at Norm and kept yelling. "Turtell, he was supposed to have our backs."

Norm pointed to the other side of the room where the front door remained opened and we could see an ambulance moving away. The three federal agents walked in, closed the door and headed in our direction.

"They don't look happy," Norm said.

"I'll show them not happy!" I walked to meet the agents, pushing Norm's hand away as he tried to stop me. I still wore the bandolier and carried the shotgun.

A Bad Combination When Life is at Stake
Chapter THIRTY-FIVE

FBI Agent Parks appeared to be arguing with the two other federal agents, Hubbard and Craig. As I approached, they shut up. Craig stepped forward before I got close enough to tear into Parks.

"What the fuck did Norm have you do?" He stared at my bandolier and shotgun. "Dragon's Breath! They aren't even legal in Florida!"

"I got a feeling there's a lot of illegal things going on." My voice raised a pitch too high.

"Beyond your understanding," Craig shouted, red in the face, as if I'd kicked him in the groin.

"What we did, without any help from you assholes," I yelled, "is get your agent out before he got beat to death!"

"What you did, shit-for-brains," Craig shot back, "is destroy two years of surveillance work. What we needed to nail those bastards is now ash, thanks to you!"

Parks walked between us. "You didn't want to discuss your program with Norm," Parks said to Craig. "No way they knew what you needed."

"And no one knew they planned to burn down the damn building!" Craig continued to shout. "Don't think this will go unnoticed, Parks. It goes into my report." Craig and Hubbard walked outside and left the door open.

"Sorry about that," Parks said.

"Where was Turtell? He was supposed to be there to back us up!" I hadn't lowered my voice.

"Quiet down, Murphy." Parks looked past me and I realized we had everyone's attention.

"My friend got shot in the parking lot." I lowered my voice but not my anger. "The man I'm after was on the motorcycle that got away. Turtell was supposed to see that didn't happen."

Norm placed his hand on my shoulder and caught me off guard. "We need to talk, Mick."

"Parks needs to talk. That's what I need." I turned back to Parks.

"Thank you for saving my agent. I appreciate what all of you did and maybe I can help you get Morgan." Parks walked away.

Norm pushed me in the same direction.

Reacting when angry, Norm had often told me, only makes things worse, clouds your judgment. I thought of that as we walked together, but my anger still boiled. Texas Rich could've been killed because Parks' sniper wasn't where he was supposed to be. I wanted an explanation and doubted anything said would still my anger.

We stopped at the table with the blueprints for the Tit-4-Tat.

"There are things you aren't aware of, Mick," Norm said when we stopped.

"Yeah! Make me aware of Turtell," I said.

"After Agent Turtell neutralized the bikers outside, he went to his location on the river." Parks said this as an explanation. Nice and tidy, the word *neutralized*. Reads better on reports than *murdered in cold blood*. It didn't make me any less angry. "A dozen bikers went to the old fish camp. Others headed toward the Panhandle and a few went to the Florida-Georgia border." Parks looked at me as if he were reading my mind. "Morgan is at the fish camp."

"How do you know?" It sounded too contrite.

"Turtell saw him arrive. Called me." Parks looked at Norm. "You want to tell him?"

"Mick doesn't believe in coincidence." Norm grinned. "Something about his days as a journalist."

"Try me!" I said.

Norm rubbed his nose and then his chin as if he were

stroking a goatee. "The FBI isn't aware of this." Norm hesitated, but I understood what *this* meant. "The DEA and ATF operation is good. They've gotten this far because they piggybacked on Parks' long-term investigation of the Rattlers. Long-term because he had someone inside."

"The man you brought out?" I didn't know how this affected me.

Norm nodded. "Yeah. The men behind desks in D.C. didn't want to interfere with the DEA/ATF investigation and, basically, wrote off the undercover agent."

"Not with my approval," Parks said. "Not to my liking."

"I knew Parks was up here, off the books. And when you told me Morgan rode with the Rattlers, it all clicked. I reached out and asked if I could do anything," Norm said.

"If you knew the Rattlers had your agent, why not just go in and get him?" I said.

"A couple of reasons. We needed proof to get a warrant, you didn't. No one involved showed any willingness to get a warrant. I'm not here, officially, so I couldn't get one. Washington wouldn't allow it. Too early in their investigation," Parks said. "The fact that I'm off the books on this, and only have a few volunteers helping, keeps me on the sidelines, watching and waiting. A bad combination when someone's life is at stake."

"When I called," Norm broke in, "I was aware of the situation, but I didn't understand the intensity of it. I didn't expect to involve you or the others."

"Coincidence?" I said.

"When Parks told me his plan, I knew Pauly and Bob could handle it."

"What about me?"

"I kept Bob with you, Pauly with Texas Rich and Burt with me," Norm said. "As it turned out, everyone did their job like pros."

"Thanks to the vests, no one's dead." I tapped my chest. I

still wore the vest.

"Vests we had in the cars," Parks said. "Flash bangs, Craig or Hubbard wouldn't get for us. I asked."

"If you're off the FBI books on this, aren't you screwed when he files his report?" Craig's last words came to mind.

"I, or I should say you men saved an agent's life. I don't care what Craig writes in his report." Parks grinned. "But, I will remind him that he knew I worked without consent and for two months he went along with it. I get called on the carpet, I have no problem telling the truth."

"So, if I understand, you don't have the manpower to go into the fishing camp. The other night or today."

"What you see is what I have." Parks looked around the dark room. Most everyone stood by the back window watching the Tit-4-Tat burn. "Agents Frank Toppino, retired Miami Bureau Chief, believes like I do about taking care of your own. Pat Labrada, Tom Sireci, Steve Hansen and I work together in the Miami office. They're on vacation. A few more men I've worked with, too. I took their help but I couldn't put their lives in danger."

"But ours . . ."

"Norm assured me . . ."

"No back up if we needed it. Not even from next door," I said.

Norm and Parks shook their heads.

"And if we got caught . . .?"

"You knew that going in, hoss," Norm said. "Now, you wanna move ahead and talk about the fish camp?"

"Pauly's hurt, Texas Rich is wounded and out of the game. It was going to be impossible with six of us. How are we going to do it with four?"

"Maybe Turtell could help." Parks smirked. "He's in place and you know he's a good shot."

"Maybe some volunteers along the road?" Norm said.

"Possible," Parks said. "I'll help but I have to ask the

others."

I Thought the Angels Would Protect Us
Chapter THIRTY-SIX

Firefighters still poured water on what remained of the Tit-4-Tat, its smoldering ruins sending spirals of white smoke into the night sky. Police officers, probably detectives because many wore suits, hovered around the four tarp-covered bodies, stepping over fire hoses and avoiding tireless firefighters.

Uniformed cops kept spectators away and directed traffic. The fire inspectors hadn't gone through the Tit-4-Tat's skeletal remains yet, so the authorities had no idea what waited for them.

Parks promised to meet us at the St. Johns River in the morning and then we could make plans about Morgan's capture. Parks was tired. We were all tired. Tomorrow would arrive soon enough.

Texas Rich's arm stayed in a sling. No one seemed to know who took care of the wound or gave him shots and a bottle of painkillers. It all happened while I argued with Parks.

We left the scene and drove back to the motel, excited to be alive. It didn't take long for the gruesome possibility that we could have been the ones dead and burnt to crush our exhilaration. We finished the ride in silence. I reflected on the longest four or five minutes of my life, and how it could've ended.

Padre Thomas leaned against the railing outside Norm's room, smoking, looking in the direction we'd come from. Had he watched the flames and smoke? It was two in the morning and he looked like he hadn't slept since we sent him back. I wondered if he'd eaten anything since the pizza slices at the stakeout.

We gathered at Norm's room, weary from it all, to have a

last beer before sleep. Pauly showed off bruises on his chest from when the bullet, or if you believed him bullets, hit the vest and knocked him down. Pauly and Bob helped Texas Rich to his room and a pill induced sleep. Burt took his unfinished beer with him.

Padre Thomas stood outside, smoking, looking into the night sky. Seeing what? Angels?

"What do you think Parks has planned for us?" My warm beer remained untouched.

"No idea, Mick." Norm yawned, a quiet admittance to the need for sleep. "I think he can give us updated intel and that's it. The planning is our responsibility."

I poured the beer in the sink and trashed the bottle. "This needs to end, Norm." I looked toward Padre Thomas and still wondered what he saw in the night.

"That's easy enough." Norm stayed by the kitchen counter. "Call the FDLE, tell them where Morgan is and let them handle it."

"I don't mean that." I turned to face him. "I mean you and me."

The fire, the heat, the smoke and the death of the night had frustrated me. I didn't realize the toll it had taken until Norm's words came out naturally, casually, and I couldn't connect the way he spoke to the grisly evening that had recently ended and almost killed us. Killed me! I didn't want to die.

Norm might have been tired and that could have been the reason for his bizarre expression. "You and me?"

"Yeah." I yawned. "I need a break. A long break."

"From me?"

I nodded. "Every time you show up in Key West, the shit flies thick. I'm tired of it. You show up. Violence follows." The words rushed out and I could see from his expression they hurt.

"Hold on, hoss!" Norm raised his voice, as his hands shot

into the air, palms out, letting me know I should stop. "I came with a woman on vacation. You got me involved in this. Not the other way around." His tone of voice carried hurt and anger.

"I know." My voice low, hiding my embarrassment. "But it's the whole picture, now. It's taken years to paint and I don't like it. I don't like my involvement in it and you're the common denominator."

"Okay, we leave in the morning." Norm leaned against the counter, his voice under control but his peculiar expression said differently. I realized that my comments had hurt him and that hurt had turned into a controlled anger. I had found the chink in his armor and it was our friendship. "We don't have to meet Parks or get Morgan. You call Richard, he'll call the FDLE. Let them get Morgan. We'll be in Key West by early afternoon and I can finish my date and you can go on with your life and I'll be out of your way."

"You pissed?"

"Disappointed."

"I made a promise to Robin." I almost whispered the words. I had just told my best friend I didn't want him around any longer and now I was about to ask him for one more favor. "We get Morgan tomorrow, if you'll help."

"You want to be the one to drag his ass back to Key West."

"Something like that, yeah."

Norm stretched, bent down, touched his toes, paused and then came straight up, something he often did when bone-tired. "When I help a friend, I finish the job."

The words were curt and sent me the message he wanted them to, *I don't abandon a friend.*

"We meet Parks at the river in the morning?"

"We'll leave at eight. I need some sleep." Norm walked to the door, my sign to leave.

Padre Thomas greeted me with a sad, half grin as Norm

closed the door.

"I was glad to see everyone came back." He crushed his cigarette butt under his foot. There had to be a whole package of crushed butts there.

"You mad because we made you leave?" I headed for my room and Padre Thomas tagged along.

"No," he whispered. "I understand. I need to talk with you, Mick."

"About tomorrow?" I opened the door and we went into my room.

"Yes." He looked for an ashtray but he knew we were in non-smoking rooms. "If I asked you not to go, to let the authorities handle Morgan, would you?"

I shook my head. "I can't make that decision until I hear what the FBI tells me tomorrow."

Padre Thomas stayed quiet. It had become unsettling, this new side of him. I missed the opinionated, chain-smoking, Budweiser drinker.

"I can go with you in the morning?"

"Sure, but you have to do what I say."

"I'll stay on the sidelines. Maybe wait at the river restaurant."

"I have no idea what's going to happen, Padre," I said. "We may be going back to Key West and let the cops get Morgan. So, you could get your wish."

"No," he said. "If you go to the river, you'll want to get Morgan. You made Robin a promise."

"Yes, I did." He knew without my ever mentioning the promise to him. I didn't want to explore the possibilities of angels, so I didn't ask.

"You think it matters to her now?"

"It matters to me."

"So, this is about you?"

His words surprised me. "Padre, it's about Robin. It's about what Morgan did to Robin. And it's about my promise to her not let him get away with it."

"No, Mick, it's about you," he said. "You will kill him."

"You don't know that! I want to bring him to Key West. I want him to get what he deserves for what he did."

"Call the authorities, call Richard and you'll be responsible for Morgan's arrest and have kept your promise," he said. "Go after him and you will kill him and maybe hurt yourself, your soul."

"I thought the angels would protect you and me." What I hoped to be light and jesting words, didn't come out that way. They sounded like a challenge.

"They can't protect us from ourselves, Mick." He gave me another half grin and left.

You Know Much About Meth?
Chapter THIRTY-SEVEN

In the morning, we paired up and left in the same vehicles we'd came in on Monday. Texas Rich insisted on coming and when he showed us he really didn't need the sling, pain shot across his body and he stooped.

"Hey, it's my left arm, I shoot with my right." He tried to smile as he put his arm back in the sling but the pain won out.

He swore he'd stay with Padre Thomas. He might have believed it. None of us did.

The overcast sky promised cold, damp weather. If it dropped another ten degrees, it could snow. *Well Toto, we're not in Key West any longer.* So much for sunny, warm Florida.

The parking lot at the Astor Marina had a few pickup trucks in it, four cars that screamed FBI, and all but three slips held boats. The river mirrored the weather, with choppy, granite-colored water and a rushing southbound current.

Griff stood outside the restaurant, smoking his pipe and looking as if he wore the same outfit as when we last saw him. He watched as we parked in different locations of the lot but didn't acknowledge us with a nod or a wave.

"Your credit card went through." White smoke came from the pipe's bowl as Griff spoke to Pauly. "You goin' to ruin a few more of my boats today?"

"Never can tell," Pauly said.

"Your money's good here." He smirked and gave Pauly a wink.

"Maybe after breakfast."

"Try the grits, they're good, too." Griff never took his stare off Pauly. "Men inside look like they might be waitin' on y'all." He knocked his pipe against a wood post to rid it of ashes and walked away.

Inside Agent Parks, Turtell and four others from last night sat at the restaurant's largest table. It wasn't big enough for all of us, but we made do and sat down. The kitchen's warmth and smells of frying bacon, sausage and eggs eddied around, helping push aside the bad memories from last night. We ordered coffee and breakfast.

"The fire marshal is going through the building later this morning." Parks started talking. "The second story collapsed late last night."

"Done with that." Norm sipped his coffee. He didn't care about yesterday. He wanted Morgan and then to get on with his life without me. He turned to Turtell. "What can you tell us?"

Turtell looked at Parks, who nodded.

"About a dozen Rattlers at the cabin," he said.

"Morgan? Is he one of them?" I said.

"Yeah. I saw him this morning, early," Turtell said. "They've set up a perimeter about a quarter mile from the cabin, facing the access road. Two men. Then another two about a half mile down."

"What about from the waterside?" Norm asked for more coffee.

"It's mostly marsh. The solid ground is narrow where they dock and there are two men watching that from the fire pit area." Turtell sighed and drank coffee. "Security counts for six of the twelve. Something interesting, though."

"What's that?" Norm looked between Turtell and Parks.

"The past days I've watched them, men brought firewood to the pit." Turtell looked at Parks, but Parks remained neutral. "Nobody's bringing wood this morning."

"Meaning what?" I said.

"I'm only guessing, but I think they're planning to bug out today, so no beer and fire tonight."

"What are the others doing?" Norm said.

"In and out." Turtell looked uncomfortable. Too much time confined to the sniper spot; he didn't know how to handle the extra space around him. "That's how I spotted Morgan. They came outside to have a smoke."

"Light up inside," Parks said and raised his arms, "Boom! Flick your bic and the place goes up."

No one responded. "You know much about meth?"

"It kills the user," I said.

"Poor man's speed," Norm said.

"Yeah, to both." Parks looked at his group around the table. I could tell they thought we were stupid. Maybe we were. "You can snort or smoke it. The first time it hits your pleasure receptors wow! There's nothing like it. I'm told, I haven't tried it. The Bureau has researchers come in to talk to us about it."

"The user is chasing that first time high," said Agent Toppino. We'd met him and the other three agents last night. "The high feels beautiful, and the user doesn't think about, or maybe doesn't know that he or she will be dead in six months."

"The reason they don't smoke inside," Parks went on, "is the chemicals they're cooking are toxic and the fumes very ignitable. Usually, the meth labs move constantly because the smell gets too strong and the garbage dangerous when it backs up."

"The Rattlers like this cabin because the river breeze helps dissipate the smell," Toppino said, "and they dump the garbage into the river and the current moves it away."

"Is the cabin approachable?" I didn't care about meth. I wanted Morgan.

Turtell looked around the table. "This it?"

"Less two of us," Norm said.

"Plus five of us." Parks pointed at his agents. "All volunteers. I was willing to come alone."

Heads nodded all around.

"You know how dangerous this is turning out to be, right?" Norm finished his coffee.

Parks looked at his agents again. "It's personal, Norm."

Norm waited.

"Our agent died last night," Parks said. "Never regained consciousness."

"You'll never know how they caught on to him," Norm said. "We left him hogtied with the others."

"Maybe Morgan knows, so now we've got personal reasons to help." Parks looked at Turtell.

"They're heavily armed." Turtell began at Parks' request. "Automatic rifles and who knows what else. Ten of you against twelve of them."

"Can't you change those numbers?" Norm grinned at Turtell.

"By two for sure." He smiled back. "You coming in on the waterside?"

"The only thing I know for sure is we won't be dropping in by helicopter," Norm said as our breakfast came.

"If they're leaving today . . ." I began to say.

"Tonight," Turtell said. "They move the meth at night by boat. They go south. I don't know where to."

Parks cleared his throat. "It might be time we take this outside. I've got a map."

"Thanks for breakfast." Norm stood. "Follow us to Bob's pickup and we'll talk."

Morgan Could be Inside
Chapter THIRTY-EIGHT

Outside, the dark clouds looked heavy with rain and moved sluggishly across the sky. Though the wind had slackened off, it felt colder. We waited by Bob's pickup. Parks and his crew of dissident agents joined us. He used the tailgate of the truck and spread out a few pages of hand- drawn maps. The rough sketches copied onto eight-by-ten paper.

"Agent Phillips drew these." Parks didn't have to tell us Agent Phillips had been his inside source that Norm had pulled from the Tit-4-Tat. "I had them enlarged on the office copy machine."

In this day of computers, it surprised me that the FBI still used copy machines.

Parks chose a sketch that showed the directions to the cabin from Route 17. He pointed at a squiggly line. "This dirt road, more an overgrown path really, is hard to spot, unless you know where to look. We've driven by."

Norm pushed next to Parks, moving us aside. "How far to the cabin?"

"Give or take, a mile, mile and a quarter off the road." Parks ran his finger along the crooked line that showed the way to the cabin.

"Any other way in?" Norm turned to Turtell.

"Waterside," he said.

"From Route 17, it's pretty much overgrown all around." Parks ran his finger around the sketch. "No other way in without making noise."

"If security consists of two men a half mile from the cabin and another two a quarter mile," Norm pointed at the squiggly line, "their whole purpose is to be a warning alarm. Four men couldn't stop a police raid. Why an alarm?"

"Slow down the cops, give the cabin crew the extra few

minutes to escape on the water with the product," Parks said.

"Escape after blowing the cabin," Norm said. "Another diversion, an extra few minutes to get away. Less evidence left behind."

"That's a possibility," Parks said.

"If we've got to go in during the day, we go in from the water, we blow the cabin." Bob pulled the sketch that showed the waterside, his Navy SEAL training kicking in. "Wham, bam, thank you ma'am ."

Norm took the sketch from Bob and put it on top of the other drawings. "Morgan could be inside."

"Okay. Once up close, circle the cabin. Are these the exits?" Bob pointed at the sketch of the cabin.

"Yes." Parks indicated the Xs on the drawings. "Exits at the front and back, facing into the woods, away from the water and road."

"We've got enough people to cover the exits," Bob said. "Call for Morgan to surrender or we blow the cabin with everyone in it."

"What about the four men watching the road in?" I said.

Bob looked toward Turtell. "Can you move and cover the road?"

"Take me a half hour," he said. "But I can."

Norm turned to Parks. "What do you have for weapons?"

"M4s." Parks pointed to the three FBI sedans near the restaurant.

"Do the bikers break routine for lunch?" Norm directed his question to Turtell.

Turtell shook his head. "One or two come out at a time, eat a sandwich, drink a beer, down by the river, away from the stench, take a smoke."

"On a time schedule?" Norm said.

"Not that you'd notice," Turtell said. "Twelve, one o'clock, somewhere in there."

"So, at around noon, we have six workers inside the meth

lab and six outside covering the perimeter." Norm looked between Parks and Turtell. "One or two come out and go to the fire pit to eat. That's four out in the open." He turned to Turtell.

"It's not impossible," he said before Norm asked about taking out the four. "I can do that and then change locations to cover the four on the dirt road."

"Have to be quick, so one of 'em doesn't get off a warning shot," Bob said and Turtell nodded.

Norm turned to Bob. "How would you do the water approach?"

"If security is neutralized, I'd come in by boat, deploy toward the cabin, circle it." Bob looked around. "Two maybe three boats. Two come in and one covers our backs."

"Someone drives the boat, I can cover your backs!" Texas Rich had been looking for a way to get involved. "Or I can drive the boat. It frees up a man."

"You have boats?" Parks scanned the slips.

"Not yet. Padre Thomas, you have to stay at the marina." Norm looked into the group. "You have anyone that can handle a boat?"

"I can drive a boat," Padre Thomas said before Parks answered. "Sailboats I'm not comfortable with, but motorboats are okay."

Norm turned to me and I shook my head.

"Mick, you and me, we find the old man." Norm walked away without waiting for an answer.

"He's got an office where the restaurant ends." I caught up with Norm and turned him away from the docks.

Griff must have seen us coming because he walked outside, stopped, lit his pipe and met us. He looked toward Bob's pickup. "Three boats, again?"

"Has to hold five, six people." Norm wasn't a water person, he didn't know what to ask for.

"Follow me." Griff walked toward the docks. He turned

away from what I thought would be his rental boats and went to the large boats.

He stopped at what I guessed to be a 32-foot Chris Craft. A man and woman sat in the stern drinking coffee.

"Like it?" Griff grinned. "A '62, 32-foot Roamer. Steel hull." His grin widened. "Thought that might interest you." He walked to the boat, we followed. "Bob and Fran, Decker, everyone calls him Decker. These men might be interested in a short-term rental of your boat."

Decker and Fran stood up and walked to the rail. She wore a paint-stained smock, he was barefoot in shorts and a T, even with the cold. They said hello.

"Boat's not for rent, you know that Griff," Decker said.

"These are the men I mentioned the other day." He spoke as if his words were in code and the couple perked up.

"That's a different story." Decker welcomed us aboard.

"Griff, what's going on here?" I stayed on the dock and Norm followed my lead.

Griff laughed. "Decker's secret is he's retired CIA. No big secret along the water."

Decker toasted us with his coffee cup.

"Fran, she's become a local celebrity artist," Griff said. "Rents a small space on the top floor and paints." He pointed toward the restaurant. "Some beautiful ones and some baffle the hell out of me but she sells 'em at our artists' craft shows."

"I think there's been a mistake." Norm backed up a few steps. "We needed a fishing boat."

"Sure you do," Decker said. "And I need more coffee, so why don't you come onboard and we can talk about what you're fishing for."

Pretty Sure You're Not Meth Dealers
Chapter THIRTY-NINE

Decker and his wife Fran led us into the boat's comfortable cabin. A half-pot of coffee sat on the galley stove. Decker brought it to the table. We sat and Fran gave us cups.

"We drink it black," she said as an apology for not having sugar or milk.

"Black and strong." Decker filled our cups.

We sat at the small table, not speaking.

Decker smiled. "I'm not usually the first to speak."

"I told Decker about your, um, returning my boats and the damage." Griff spoke up. "We all heard the altercation that night."

"Hard not to," Decker said. "Quiet on the water at night. The ruckus kept Fran and me up."

"Not sure what the old man told you . . ."

"Old man my ass!" Griff said to Norm and then chuckled. "If you're gonna use old man, I'd appreciate it if you put *wise* in front of it. Asian people respect their elders' wisdom, you might use that as an example."

"Griff spent a lot of time in Nam," Decker said. "We both did."

Norm's expression told me he had to decide in what direction to go. Was Griff a crazy old coot? Could Decker be retired CIA? And why did any of it matter?

"I understand your reluctance," Decker said. "I really do. So, let me tell you what I think and then you can stay or go. Okay?"

Norm nodded and sipped his coffee.

"I've been out of the Agency for five years." Decker began. "I still have contacts at Langley and other posts. What I know is the CIA has no operation involving the Rattlers, either locally or in the Panhandle."

Decker went on, the coffee pot became empty and we stayed. He matched Norm to JSOC, and Parks to the FBI, but couldn't connect them to the ongoing DEA and ATF investigations of the Rattlers. For me, he knew I had been a journalist and mentioned that our paths had crossed more than once in Mexico. What baffled me was how he knew my name.

"Griff gave me descriptions and the restaurant's surveillance cameras had good footage of you." Decker turned to Norm. "I thought he'd know."

Norm almost laughed. "I've told him, I've proven it to him, he just doesn't understand or want to believe that big brother watches."

"Watches most everyone," Decker said. "Eyes and ears of the world!"

"What's this have to do with renting three boats?" Norm said.

"Griff and I tried to think of what's going on." Decker got up and made more coffee as he talked. "This morning's news about the Tit-4-Tat burning to the ground . . ."

"And them finding multiple bodies in the ruins just now, according to the news," Griff said.

"And your showing up here this morning." Decker refreshed our coffee. "We tried to figure out how you and your crew," Decker pointed outside, "could take on the bikers. It challenged us."

Norm and I drank our coffee.

"Pretty sure you're not rival meth dealers." Decker sat down. "Can you tell us what you want to accomplish? FBI, JSOC, an ex-journalist. Damn, with this group Jimmy Breslin's going to have to write volume two of 'The Gang That Couldn't Shoot Straight.'"

"You're looking for three boats," Griff said. "So you're going in from the water. We're willing to help, but we'd like to know why you're risking your lives."

"It's your circus, hoss." Norm nodded to me. The decision of what to tell them rested on my head. Maybe this was a little payback for ending our friendship so abruptly.

I couldn't decide on how much to tell them, so I began at the beginning, with Robin's death and moved forward, skipping the Silver Slipper and the Russians.

"I had a simple plan for when we found Morgan," I said. "We would grab him with as few bikers around as possible. Obviously, it all went south."

"Mick Murphy's Law." Norm grinned. "If Murphy can fuck it up," he looked at Fran. "Sorry for my language. But if he can, he will, somehow."

Norm received smiles from everyone but me. I continued with my story, ending at our decision to go in by water. I left out a lot, including Turtell and the Dragon's Breath-caused fire at the strip club.

I finally asked, how and why their involvement.

"You don't come into my neighborhood and open a meth lab." Decker poured the last of coffee. "The stench sent Griff and me off on a search and from there it was like being back in Nam, surveillance, hide and seek. We put our intel together each night."

"And you didn't alert the authorities?" Norm finished his coffee.

"Discovered the feds were on to them," Decker said.

"Sent letters to the paper," Griff said. "Got nothing."

"So, we've been up the creek, so to say, to see the meth lab." Decker smiled. "We have an engine so we didn't care about not having a paddle."

"How far up the creek?" Norm sounded interested and that made me think he might believe these two.

"Not as far as you got with Griff's boats." Decker nodded to Fran and his wife got up and brought a rolled up nautical chart back. Decker opened it. "Here we are." He pointed at the marina and moved his finger south to the creek that led to the meth lab. "I can get about halfway in. There's dry land to the port side. Leads to their fire pit."

"They load out the meth to a boat," Griff said. "We've followed them."

"Dangerous." Norm looked at the chart. "Where did they go?"

"Late, no other boat traffic and they go to Lake Dexter." Decker showed the route to the lake south of the marina. "Seaplane lands, they load it. The plane takes off, their boat heads back here. None's the wiser."

"You done your recon," Norm said. "How big of a plane?"

"Single engine," Griff said. "Met ain't like bales of square grouper."

"You don't mess in my backyard." Decker rolled up the chart. "How can we help?"

"We'll get a call sometime after noon and then we'll want to land by the fire pit," Norm said. "Ten of us."

Decker looked out a porthole. "I count thirteen."

"One man wounded, one's a priest," Norm said. "They don't go."

"That leaves eleven." Decker wondered about Turtell, the eleventh man outside.

"You don't need to know what the other guy does." Norm said.

"I need to ask about weapons." Decker looked uncomfortable. "Anything big?"

"M4s, shotguns and sidearms," Norm said.

"Better get them aboard." Decker looked at his watch. "We'll ride by and make sure they don't have a boat in the water."

Decker followed us out. Fran kissed him on the cheek and left for her painting room.

It's Not Perfect, It's What We've Got
Chapter FORTY

"I don't like it." Parks and his agents shared concern about Decker really being retired CIA. "If I had a few days, I could ask around. Someone would know if he was ex-CIA and what his rep was. He and the old man could be two crazies living on the water. Or they could be the eyes and ears for the Rattlers."

"If he and Griff are working for the Rattlers they already know we're here," Norm said. "They don't know about Turtell, so he's our ace in this."

"I can lay down fire, if it's an ambush when you get off the boat," Turtell said. "Slow them down, give you a chance to regroup and respond."

"I need him," Parks pointed at Texas Rich, "to be on the boat, so there's no communications between Decker and the bikers after we get on land."

"I can do that!" Texas Rich couldn't hold in his excitement at finally being included.

"With one good arm?" I said. "Two guys to watch."

"I can send Labrada." Parks pointed to one of his agents. "He's quick on his feet. Even if Decker is who he says he is, we may need someone onboard for cover as we exit. This Morgan won't go peacefully."

"I can drive a boat," Padre Thomas said. "You could free up Texas Rich and Labrada."

His comment was another example of the change I'd seen in his demeanor. Padre Thomas had never been one to condone or go along with violence. Now, uncharacteristically, he offered his assistance on a daylight raid that would certainly end in the violent death of some.

"We've the weather to contend with, too." Norm pointed skyward. "By noon it could be raining. Where do they go for a smoke in the rain?"

"Only been here once when it rained," Turtell said. "They set up a tarp by the fire pit. Had old chairs for them to sit in."

"Big tarp or like someone would use in their backyard?"

"I don't know." Turtell hunched his shoulders. "Maybe ten or twelve square feet."

"If they're buggin' out, let's hope they still do that," Norm said.

"If they're smokers, they'll have to," Parks said. "No one's going to let anyone smoke next to the lab. It's dangerous enough, as it is."

"Which begs the question." I looked toward Parks and his crew. "Why bother with more meth if the whole operation is in danger? After last night, they've gotta figure something's up."

"That's one of those questions we don't have an answer to," Parks said.

"Why's Morgan even involved in it?" Norm looked at me. "I can understand why the Rattlers would be interested in his blackmail scheme, but why involve him in the meth operation?"

"We'll ask him when we get him," I said. "We should put the weapons onto the boat before it rains."

"Labrada." Parks pointed at one of his men. "Take Sireci with you and board the boat. Introduce yourselves, be polite and observant."

The two agents nodded and left.

"Not a trusting soul, are you Parks?" Norm slapped him on the back.

"Why I've lived this long, Norm. I wish we were better armed." Parks faced Norm. "In the daylight, we could use 37mm grenades with buckshot, set that cabin ablaze and spook the hell out of them."

"We can't even get flash-bangs," Norm said. "Because you're off the books?"

"I can't requisition anything." Parks' face tightened. "We've got vests because they were in the cars. That's the best I can offer. Sorry."

"They worked for us last night, nothing to be sorry about." Norm picked up the copied sketches. "We should've Google mapped this area. Hindsight."

"I should go." Turtell walked to Parks. "I'll call you when two come out and join the two at the fire pit. If it's a go, I will put them down so you can come in. Rain could work against us."

"You think it will go that easy? Even in rain?" Norm said.

"I have to decide whether to move closer or not." Turtell looked at the darkening sky. "Showers, I'm okay. A downpour I need to get closer. I have a suppressor for the rifle. Add the rain, it benefits me, covers whatever little noise is left and might confuse them for a moment when the first man goes down." Turtell walked toward his car.

"How long's he been a Bureau sniper?" Norm watch Turtell walk away.

"He's not," Parks said. "He's freelance."

Norm looked wary of Parks' words. "Since when has the Bureau used freelance?"

"It might surprise you Norm, but your agency isn't the only one that does things off the books."

Norm looked doubtful but let Parks' comment go. "We've got our weapons. Let's get 'em on the boat."

We all began to disperse.

Parks stopped Norm. "I'm not comfortable with this."

"I know. It's not perfect but it's what we've got."

"Give me twenty-four hours to run this guy down . . ."

"We might not have six hours." Norm looked skyward. "And the rain isn't going to make it any easier."

"I need some time with Morgan," Parks murmured. "You understand?"

"Yeah. Break him fast, Parks. Maybe Decker, if he was

really CIA back in Nam, can help with that." Norm walked away.

Eight of Us Are Going In
Chapter FORTY-ONE

Padre Thomas walked with Norm and me.

"You don't wanna come with us, Padre." I pulled the duffel bag of weapons from the Jeep.

"I need to, Mick." He offered a desolate smile, as if he had no say in the decision. "You may need me."

I didn't like that. Did he know something I didn't? What did the angels tell him? When I thought that, I stopped cold. This was no time to think about the Padre's angels, real or imagined. I had to focus.

"Unless you can walk on water, Padre Thomas, once the boat leaves the dock, you aren't going anywhere," Norm said.

"I know." Padre Thomas kept the woeful smirk.

A light drizzle began as we approached the boat. Labrada and Sireci helped pull the group's weapons onto the aft section and then Decker and Griff moved them below. Thirteen of us left very little room to maneuver on deck.

Parks introduced himself to Decker and told him we wouldn't move until he received a phone call. Decker wanted to make one slow run up the river, past the creek, to make sure nothing waited to surprise us. He'd leave after the phone call.

Soon after boarding, the rain came down heavy. Parks held his cell phone as if willing it to ring.

The boat had been ready to go, shore power and water disconnected and only bow and aft lines kept us at the dock.

Norm and I were on deck when we heard our names called. We went below. Parks and Decker stood by the chart table looking down at a laptop image.

"Google Earth." Parks pointed at the screen.

"It's not real time," Decker said. "If I'd known a few days

ago, I might have been able to get satellite feeds. Though I'm sure with this cloud cover satellite images would be useless."

I knew that Google Earth didn't offer real time images and all the live satellite images would have shown were clouds. We looked at the best available image.

Decker and Griff took turns pointing out the old fishing camp cabin, the dirt path in, the fire pit and river. The trees and brush around the cabin made the narrow path the only access in from the main road. The creek led from the Saint Johns River and all around it showed thick brush and marsh.

Parks' phone rang. "Talk to me." He listened. "Half hour." Parks put the phone away. "Be another half hour."

"The missing man from the parking lot," Decker said.

"Need to know." Parks kept a stern expression.

Decker nodded his understanding.

"There are two forward positions." Parks pointed at the laptop. "A quarter mile from the cabin and a half mile. Where would you put them?"

"Some downed trees here." Griff pointed at the screen with his unlit pipe. "That's about a half mile. Good cover." He moved his pipe along the screen toward the cabin. "Brush here thins out. Could've dug a ditch. The ground's soft."

"Will there be a problem?" Decker said.

"Hope not," Parks answered.

Decker wanted to know what we were up against, exactly.

Parks told him about the twelve bikers. Six outside and six inside. He pointed to the cabin as it appeared on Google Earth. "Two exits. One in back, the other in front, facing the forest."

"You want me or Griff to go ashore too?"

Parks looked at Norm. He shook his head.

"Eight of us are going in," Norm said. "You and Griff need to stay with the boat. Labrada and Texas Rich are our backup."

Decker looked at Padre Thomas. I guessed his CIA

training had helped him determine who didn't belong.

"Thomas steers the boat if we need you and Griff to help us," Norm said. "Our plan is to bring out one man."

"Friendly?" Decker said.

Norm shook his head. "Important that he's alive, is all."

The rain beat down on the cabin like ball bearings falling from the sky, a cousin to the squalls that hit Key West from the Gulf of Mexico. Sometimes they're brief, just passing through and sometimes not.

"Can you get NOAA weather?" I said. Why not see a weather map of current conditions.

Decker left Google Earth and went to the weather ap. A large cloud covering Daytona showed up on the screen. Decker moved the curser across to Astor, then enlarged the map area. All around were lightning strikes, but off to the west the clouds lightened, suggesting showers. As we looked at the screen, a loud boom exploded above us.

"Lightning's here." Decker laughed.

"Do you think?" Norm motioned for Parks and me to follow him on deck.

We stood by the wheel at the captain's seat. Others moved into the cabin or under the overhang to keep out of the downpour.

"Do you know what Turtell is shooting?" Norm had some experience being a sniper in South America and I could see the weather concerned him. "He's moving locations, right? The phone call."

"Yeah," Parks said. "He needs a half hour to get in place."

We all looked at our wristwatches. It was almost noon.

"He has a Marine M40."

"Shoots a .308 round." Norm nodded to himself and looked at the rain. "In this rain he could take his shots within three-hundred yards."

"Know what he shoots, have no idea where he's going," Parks said. "What do you think?"

"We're in control of the boat, so that's good," Norm said. "Rain slows down, that's good. It doesn't and we may have trouble. We need those two guys to come out for a smoke or lunch, for any reason."

"If they don't, Turtell can still take out the waterside two, maybe even the perimeter guys." Parks counted on his fingers. "That's half."

"Better than nothing," Norm said.

Parks' cell rang. "Yeah, how far?" He listened. "We're gonna run the river a little and then get in place." He listened. "I'll call you. You're on vibrate, right?" Parks laughed. "I know you're not stupid. I'm nervous, that's all. Call you soon." He put his phone away. "Decker!" Parks yelled to overcome the rain. "Ready to go."

Decker started the engine. Griff tossed off the bow and aft lines. The boat moved cautiously out into the swift current.

He Went Face First into the Ground
Chapter FORTY-TWO

Decker kept the Chris Craft's engine running a little above idle for steering control and let the current move the boat along. Red and green running lights flickered dimly from the starboard and port sides. White bow and stern anchor lights had little effect penetrating through the curtain of rainy gloom, but the Coast Guard rules required them. That some authority might patrol the river during a storm turned into one of those chances we had to take but we didn't need to add to the reasons for them to board us.

"Approaching, on the starboard side." Decker put the engine in reverse, slowing the boat's forward motion, allowing us a few seconds to stare into the murkiness of the creek. "I don't see any lights up there." The engine whined as Decker put it into neutral and the current moved the boat. "Too dangerous to stop and anchor in this weather," he said to Parks and moved the throttle out of neutral. "Make your phone call and let's do this."

The outline of the tree stump showed itself, surrounded by rain and haze. Looking past the stump I couldn't tell a creek hid in the shadows. The heavy downpour gave way to a lighter, steady rain that beat hollows into the dark river. Lightning flashes lit up in the distance, toward Daytona and had no effect on the river. Soft, reflective booms of thunder followed but the sound grew dimmer as the flashes moved into the Atlantic.

A late afternoon sky hid behind the clouds or maybe the heavens had disappeared entirely. With the cloud cover, it was impossible to tell. Parks made his call. His voice low. The conversation brief. He nodded toward Decker and the ex-CIA agent increased the engine's speed and turned the boat around into the current, toward the invisible creek.

Bob and Pauly went onto the bow as Decker shut off the running lights and turned the boat into the hidden passageway. Visibility, with the rain, averaged about ten feet. Decker could see the hand and arm signals coming from the bow and Bob and Pauly saw far enough ahead to give directions.

Decker slowed the engine even more as he watched the depth finder. "Close to hitting bottom. Tell them to tie off to something."

Norm moved into the rain and went to the bow. Bob grabbed onto a sturdy tree limb, pulled the boat closer to shore and tied off the bowline to a tree trunk. Decker put the engine in neutral.

"Can you turn around in here?" I looked at the narrow creek.

"When the shooting starts, the boat will be turned. He can help." Decker pointed toward Padre Thomas. "You know how to use a flare gun?"

"Yeah." Decker handed me a loaded flare gun with two extra flares.

"One flare, you're heading back, so I'm ready to move." Decker pointed into the rainy sky. "Two, you're in trouble. Me and Griff will come and see what we can do."

"Three?" I looked at him.

"It means you're fucked and I should run for it."

"Got all your bases covered." I hoped Decker had a sense of humor regarding the third flare.

Norm, Pauly and Bob climbed down from the bow, soaked, as we all would be in a few minutes. Quietly, we got our weapons. Pauly and I had the shotguns and bandoliers of Dragon's Breath shells. We also carried an M4 and extra magazines. My Sig snuggled into its holster in my back. The flares and flare gun hanging out of my jacket's pocket. I felt ready for the apocalypse.

We moved onto soggy land. Texas Rich, Labrada and

Padre Thomas stayed onboard with Decker and Griff.

"Stay close," Parks said. He let Norm lead the way.

We walked single file, Bob guarding our rear. The rain fell lightly, but soaked me through in less than a couple of steps. I'd put the bandolier inside my jacket to keep the shotgun shells dry. Everyone's M4 pointed toward the ground so water didn't leak into the barrel.

My eyes adjusted to the grayness and little by little, the surroundings emerged. When Norm raised his arm in the air, we all stopped. He signaled for us to wait where we stood.

Ahead, two of the Rattlers' security men sought shelter from the rain beneath a large tree. Rifles hung from their shoulders as they smoked. Muffled words carried on the rain but were not understandable. Norm pointed to Parks, who bent over to keep the rain off his cell and dialed. I couldn't hear him.

We all watched the two men. Suddenly, one man fell back against the tree. The other grabbed him before he fell to the ground but pulled away frightened. He looked around, startled, wondering where the shot came from. He knelt on the damp ground and brought his rifle up to a firing position. He tumbled sideways, his face buried in the ground.

I didn't hear the shots. Obviously, Turtell was close by and doing what he did best.

Norm had us wait while he moved cautiously toward the two fallen men. He took handguns from their waistbands and tossed them into the woods and then picked up the rifles and signaled us forward.

"See if they have extra magazines," Norm whispered to Bob. He gave Parks one of the rifles.

"Shit!" Parks griped. "Fully automatic!"

Bob took a magazine from each man's jacket and gave one each to Norm and Parks. "I found this too." Bob held a small radio.

Norm took it. "Gives us an advantage. We'll know what

they're talking about."

"You don't know the names if a call comes?" Parks pointed to the corpses.

"Don't have to," Norm said. "Play static back and maybe they'll come out to see what's wrong."

Parks nodded. "Worth a try."

Off in the distance, maybe fifty yards away, small patches of light from the cabin showed through the rain. There was no reason to look for cover, there wasn't a dry part of me.

"Bob, you come with me. Everyone else, stay quiet." Norm and Bob headed toward the cabin's light.

They returned a few minutes later.

"That cabin is solid logs and mortar. Two stories. A-frame loft on the second floor. Stone chimney with white smoke coming out of it on this side. " Norm stood between us. "We've got nothing that'll penetrate whole logs."

"Windows?" Parks said. "The fireplace is working?"

Norm nodded. "Smoke coming out of it."

"There can't be a meth lab in there." Parks sounded upset.

"Two windows in the loft and two on the first floor." Norm ignored Parks. "Pushed out and held open with sticks. Doors are open too."

"Airing the place out, fireplace going for heat," Parks sighed. "Means they've dismantled the meth lab, since the fire didn't blow it all to hell."

"Which means?" I said.

"If they've been airing it out since last night, it's not as flammable as if they were cooking meth."

"Why do that? After last night, why not run for it?" It didn't make sense to me to take the time to clean up something you could've easily burned down. "Where's the meth lab equipment and materials?"

"My guess is that they like the location and want to come back," Parks said. "Isolated area, useable for the long term, and on the water. Beats the hell out of moving a trailer every three to four weeks because of the stench. So, they could've gone to the trouble of burying it or moving it on a boat."

"Off the front, hidden in brush is a large metal storage shed," Norm said. "It's locked. And there's a generator off the front porch. It's not on. Two restaurant-size propane tanks on the back porch. We'll take that side." Norm got us back onto the current situation. "Our problem is the men inside, not where they've moved the lab. Parks, you go to the front but contact Turtell first."

"And do what?" Parks sounded defeated now that the meth lab could be gone.

"We've got four open windows and two open doors." Norm tapped Pauly's shotgun. "Put some Dragon's Breath in, catch something inside on fire. Then they gotta come out."

"See if Turtell has the men covering the perimeter covered," Bob said. "If not, does he need more time before we make our move?"

"Murphy has a shotgun." Parks reached out to Pauly. "Give me yours and we've got both doors covered."

Pauly gave Parks the shotgun and bandolier of shells and took the fully automatic rifle. "When this goes off, the bikers guarding the road will see and hear it."

"You need to have Turtell cover our asses," Norm said. "See if he can do that. If he can't, we've gotta do it, somehow."

Parks sought shelter under a tree and called Turtell.

Bob Twisted the Biker's Head Around
Chapter FORTY-THREE

The steady rain turned into a bothersome drizzle. Blue patches of sky showed through the breaks in the clouds to the west and headed our way. Maybe the clear skies would bring some warmth too. For all its inconvenience, the rain offered us cover while we moved toward the cabin. Parks and his three men moved toward the front. We moved to the back.

A clearing about thirty feet wide circled the cabin. After that, a variety of winter-stripped trees, evergreens and thick brush went from the river to the road without a break and as deep into the forest as I could see. Norm didn't mention the covered motorcycles to Parks. I pointed at the tarp-covered bikes. Norm smiled and said nothing. He knew the Rattlers would go for their bikes when the shooting started and that's where he wanted to be. An overhang made of wood and shingle to shelter firewood from the elements contained none.

Norm, Bob, Burt, Pauly and I crouched behind bushes opposite the back door. Shadows inside moved across the windows. Smoke curled from the chimney. We knew the meth lab had closed down, but we didn't know what the men inside were doing. Or how well armed they were. Judging from the two dead sentries' weaponry, they probably had automatic weapons.

"Can you get the shotgun blast through the door from here?" Norm whispered to me.

"No. I need to get a lot closer. Too close." I wondered why he asked, since his experience should have told him the answer. He could have been testing my resolve.

Bob grabbed Norm's arm and pointed to a ladder off to the side of the cabin that faced the dirt road. "If that ladder is good, I could get up to the chimney and clog it. Smoke them out!" The ladder lay on the ground and looked as if were made of two-by-four scraps nailed together.

Norm thought for a minute. "Clog with what?"

"I'll find something wet and stuff it in there."

"A lot of space between the ladder and chimney." Norm's eyes moved back and forth. "Lot of open space to the ladder."

"I'll cover Bob's back." Burt knelt close. "You guys cover the door."

"If someone starts shooting, forget the ladder!" Norm said. "Get to cover."

Bob and Burt are six feet. They crouched and looked like hurt deer as they ran along the brush, focused on the ladder. I had my M4 pointed toward the open back door. Pauly aimed there too, using the biker's rifle he had traded Parks for. Norm aimed the other automatic rifle, but kept his M4 close. Shotguns would be of no use this far out, the Dragon's Breath flame spread too wide to be effective at this distance. I wondered if the phosphorus pellets burned wet logs or would stick to the propane tanks. I knew they'd set the motorcycles on fire.

Inside, shadows continued to pass back and forth behind the open door and windows, making my trigger finger nervous. I knew I'd shoot the first person through the door to protect my friends.

Norm put his cell phone to his ear and listened. "We're trying something, so we've got the time. I'll get back to you." He ended the call. His voice, soft and low, showed no sign of anxiousness. "Turtell has to move locations again. Parks will let us know when he's in place."

"Will he be able to stop the perimeter guys?" My voice stayed low but I couldn't keep the angst out.

"That's the idea." While Norm spoke on the phone and to me, he never took his eyes off the cabin door.

Bob and Burt moved out of the shadows. Each grabbed an

end of the ladder and hustled across the open yard. No one noticed from inside.

The fireplace must have been the cabin's original one. A mixture of local stones in various sizes and shapes, it had a wide base that narrowed into a chimney halfway up the wall. White smoke coming from it meant that the burning wood had dried out.

Bob placed the ladder against the stones and it reached to the roof's edge. He would have to get onto the roof. Ladder in place, both men searched the yard for anything Bob could use to clog the chimney.

The radio taken from the dead biker came alive. "Anything Keller?" A static voice asked.

Norm looked at the radio and rubbed the mouthpiece against his wet jacket causing more static.

"You're not comin' in asshole," the voice shouted and stopped. "Russell, you two okay?"

"Wet and cold, Ruiz, wet and cold," Russell's static voice said.

"Powers, you and Lane still there?" Ruiz said.

"Assholes and elbows, dipshit," came back from one of them. "This almost over? I can't even keep a smoke goin'."

"Careful who you callin' dipshit, dipshit," Ruiz said. "Might leave you here. One of you check on Keller and Dillon, their radio ain't workin'."

"Fucker probably got it wet," a voice replied. "I'm goin'."

The radio went quiet.

A man walked out of the woods. A hoody, doing little good against the rain, covered his head. A rifle hung from his shoulder, barrel down. He approached the cabin's back deck and checked under the tarp. I raised my rifle. Norm pushed the barrel down. He pointed toward the chimney. Bob and Burt were nowhere in sight. The biker replaced the tarp over the motorcycles. He lit a cigarette and moved toward the river.

Bob pounced on the man as he passed the chimney. With a swiftness he must have learned in the SEALs, Bob twisted the man's head halfway around. The biker went limp before Bob let go. He dragged the body back to the side of the cabin.

"What's he doing?" I looked on as Bob seemed to be undressing the body.

Pauly laughed quietly. "He's going to use the guy's clothing to stop up the chimney."

"He'd make too much noise taking the body up and stuffing it in." Norm called Parks on the cell. "We're clogging the chimney. Be ready for them to come out." He listened. "Ten minutes, I guess. Give or take. One of the perimeter guys has been taken care of, so tell Turtell he's only looking at three along the road." More listening. "I won't have to call you. You'll see smoke and that's your signal."

"We set?" Pauly said.

"Turtell isn't in place, but we go ahead Turtell or not, when these assholes come through the door, we shoot 'em," Norm said.

"We have to be careful not to kill Morgan." It began to sound like my mantra during the last few hours. "Parks and Turtell know that, right?"

"Parks needs him too." Norm pointed to the chimney.

Bob climbed along the slanted A-frame roof, a wadded up bundle of clothing in one arm. Burt stood at the foot of the ladder, his rifle pointing toward the back door. Standing, Bob began to stuff the clothing into the chimney. Done, he went to the ladder and climbed down. Both men lay the ladder on the ground and ran to the brush making their way back to us.

"Good goin'." Pauly pointed toward the chimney. No smoke came from it. "Shouldn't be long."

"Time to spread out. Pauly, you go left, keep an eye on

the road in case Turtell can't," Norm said. "Mick, you stay close to me. We may get to use that shotgun before this is over."

Pauly went far left. Bob and Burt moved maybe ten feet away. We all watched the door.

No Shit Dick Tracy
Chapter FORTY-FOUR

I felt the sun on my face. I eagerly accepted it as a promise of warmth to come. The drizzle stopped and clouds broke in places, sun shining briefly on the wooded area, casting long shadows of the scrub oaks' winter limbs. For a moment, maybe because of the stillness, I heard the weather. Earlier, with the thunder, lightning and downpour, it sounded like rock 'n' roll drummer Richard Crooks pounding away, overriding the other instruments, exciting the audience; a steady rain setting the beat, lightning flashes adding quick brightness like a lone horn from Ken Fradley, and thunder booms equaling a wild drumming solo by Crooks. Now, with the brief reprieve, bare tree branches twitched and pine trees rustled together as a damp wind blew, causing the softer sounds of drummer Mick Kilgore using wire brush sticks to accompany an easygoing jazz tune. I escaped the damp cold by hearing music in my surroundings.

We watched the cabin. Maybe, like me, everyone expected smoke to surge out the door and windows, forcing the men inside to come running out. It didn't happen.

Norm opened his phone. "Yeah, it's done. Just a matter of time." He listened. "Wait and catch them by surprise. Now they've gotta be wondering what happened to the man they sent out. Norm nodded to himself. "Cautious, maybe. Yeah, could be on their cells too." More nods. "Don't kill Morgan, is all. Remind Turtell of that." He put the phone away. "Turtell's in place."

"Keller, what the fuck's takin' you so long?" The radio voice of Ruiz squawked. "Are you there?" He yelled so loud we heard his voice from inside the cabin. "If I come down there asshole, you'll fuckin' regret it!"

Norm opened the radio's mic and rubbed it against his

wet jacket, sending only static back to Ruiz.

An unarmed man appeared at the door. He walked onto the porch and looked toward the water. Even with the sky clearing, he couldn't see to the fire pit. He looked around the outside. We kissed the muddy ground. After scanning the area, he went back inside.

"What do you think?" I looked at Norm.

"Not sure. Maybe the fire's gone out." He stared toward the cabin. "Should've had some effect by now."

Yells came from the cabin and we watched as shadows crossed the windows toward the fireplace.

"If they can stop the fire and don't come out?"

Norm looked at me. "Then it's your turn to torch the bikes."

I didn't like that. It meant walking fifteen to twenty feet out into the open so I could use the shotgun with Dragon's Breath shells to set the bikes ablaze, and get one shot into the cabin. It would take a long fifteen to thirty seconds for the two shots and another thirty to get in and out. Maybe protective fire from everyone could shield me, but with Mick Murphy's Law working so well recently, I had my doubts. This trip, Norm had started adding Mick to the old adage Murphy's Law as a joke with Nora and Peggy in Key West. I found nothing funny about it, as it seemed lately to be the truth more often than not.

Bob hit me with a pebble. He pointed to the window closest to the fireplace. Small puffs of smoke came out.

We heard yelling from inside. Ruiz seemed in charge but everyone appeared to be shouting. As the smoke got thicker, we heard coughing between the screeches. The other window and door were clear of smoke.

Norm used hand signals to alert everyone. "If nothing else, they'll come to breathe fresh air. Be ready," he whispered to me.

We all knelt on the damp ground. I raised my M4 into

shooting position. My finger nervously touching the trigger, tapping to the beat of music only I heard. Pauly, far to my left, kept his attention on the road, ready to stop any of the three men who might come from that direction. Bob and Burt focused on the cabin door.

"Wait till a couple of them are outside," Norm said. "Some will go out the front door."

"If Parks shoots right away?"

"We shoot before we lose the element of surprise." Norm turned to me. "You gonna be okay?"

I wondered if he meant about getting close so I could use the shotgun or if he meant right now, moments before the shit hit the fan. I didn't know how to answer, so I nodded my head.

The assumption that six people were inside was just that — an assumption. Turtell said a dozen bikers had arrived the night before. Three were dead, two at the fire pit and one by the cabin's outdoor fireplace wall. That left three on perimeter watch by the road. Six inside. What if there were more? Before I could ask Norm, he tapped my shoulder and pointed toward the cabin.

Two men, coughing, walked out to the porch. Each clumsily carried a rifle. They took deep breaths and coughed, almost a dry heave. The smoke inside must have been thicker than I thought.

Four men left inside. Maybe. No shots from Parks' side of the cabin. Did anyone go out that way? I had the questions, where were the answers?

A third man stood at the doorway. Ruiz? He ordered the two to check on Keller and find out what held him up at the fire pit.

"Wait!" Ruiz yelled as the two men walked away. "Abbott, you check the pit and Hoebee get up on the roof and see what's clogging the chimney." He went back inside.

The two bikers stopped and lit cigarettes. Abbott walked

toward the water and Hoebee dragged the ladder to the fireplace. He saw the body.

"Abbott," Hoebee yelled.

Abbott turned around as Hoebee motioned him to come back. "Ruiz! Ruiz!"

Ruiz came to the door and Hoebee called him over.

Abbott knelt by the body, as if looking for a pulse or a reason the man was dead. Ruiz looked down, turned and bolted for the cabin door.

Bob and Burt shot toward the two bikers. Abbott went down quickly. Hoebee got a few wild shots off in the right direction before he went down.

Norm shot at the running Ruiz as he ducked behind the motorcycles, missing.

The cabin door closed. I hadn't fired a shot.

Still no shots fired from Parks' side.

Two rifle barrels poked out the window and let go a salvo of automatic fire in our direction. We seemed to spend a lot of time with Mother Earth in our faces. The shots went high. Now we knew they had automatic weapons. Foolishly, the inexperienced go wild with the rifles and empty magazines too quickly. How many magazines would they have inside?

The thick, weathered oak logs would stop our shots, so we all aimed toward the one window, breaking the glass and forcing the rifles to disappear. Norm motioned for me to watch the door. Bob and Burt fired intermittently at the window and that kept the shooters away.

Gunfire reports came from the other side of the cabin. Now the bikers knew we had them surrounded. It also meant Ruiz would be on his cell calling for help. I wondered if the damp weather held the reports in or did they reverberate to the marina as they had before?

A drizzle began. I looked toward the sky. Dark clouds had moved back over us. Patches of sun showed far to our west.

"They're not going to try for the bikes?" I waited for

Norm's answer.

"I wouldn't," Norm said. "Who knows what they'll do?"

The cabin door opened slowly allowing two rifles to stick out. They shot blindly at us. We fell back to Mother Nature, waiting for the magazines to empty. If they knew what they were doing, once empty, two other people would start shooting, forcing us to retreat for better cover. A few shots hit the dirt in front of us, but most flew over our heads.

Bob sent a volley of shots toward the door but its thickness kept it from doing any good.

One of Burt's shots hit a rifle barrel and we watched it pull away. The door closed.

It became so quiet I could hear the raindrops falling.

Gunshots came from the other side of the cabin.

A rifle stuck out the window and sent random shots over our heads, but this time they didn't empty the magazine. Someone organized the defense. Ruiz?

We moved further back and took shelter behind two large oaks. Pauly stayed in place. He watched the dirt road, waiting on the three bikers who guarded it.

"They're shooting to keep us occupied." Norm pointed toward the cabin.

"They've called some?" Bob guessed but we all agreed.

Norm nodded. "Problem is, are they coming on the water or from Daytona?"

"I'll go back and warn Decker," Burt said.

"Okay, but come right back," Norm said and Burt made his way through the forest toward the boat. "Mick, we can't wait any longer."

"I can get close enough to use the shotgun," Bob said. "No reason for Mick to chance that."

"I'll do it." I hoped the anxiety I felt didn't come across. "You two lay down fire and keep them away from the window and door for two minutes. That's all I need." I knew two minutes was a long time.

"Go for the bikes," Norm said. "Can you get one shot through the window too?"

I looked at the window. Our bullets had cleared away most of the glass. "I can try."

"Bob and I will be on either side of you. You ready?"

As I listened to Norm, I took the bandolier of Dragon's Breath shell out from inside my jacket and strung it across my chest and shoulder. I made sure the shotgun had five shells loaded into it.

"I've got five shots." We walked out from behind the oak. "I'm guessing it's thirty feet to the bikes. I'm shooting when I think I'm halfway there."

"You don't have time to reload," Norm said.

"No shit Dick Tracy." I tried to joke. "The fifth shot comes with my back to the cabin. Keep your extra magazines close."

"Is he worth it?" Norm whispered.

"I made a promise. If this is what it takes to keep it, yes he's worth it."

Norm and Bob kept watch as I moved forward. No one shot from the window. An eeriness came with the quiet. Even the rain fell silently.

A hand grenade came soaring out the window.

Promise Kept
Chapter FORTY-FIVE

Before the grenade landed, I turned and ran back toward the forest. I focused on a large oak about fifty feet away. I didn't run fast enough. The drizzle and earlier downpour made the ground muddy and it slowed me.

I felt myself thrust forward by the force of the grenade's concussion and then dropped to the wet ground, before I actually heard the explosion. The thunderous eruption damaged my hearing. I dropped the shotgun. It lay in the mud ahead of me. My jacket had little tears along the sleeves. Silence surrounded me. I no longer heard the rain. I felt the drizzle on my face.

Norm lifted me up. His mouth moved but I didn't hear the words.

Pauly picked up the shotgun and moved toward the cabin. I watched as Bob and Burt fired toward the cabin, laying down fire to protect Pauly. I saw the muzzle flashes. I didn't hear the shots.

When Norm sat me down by an oak tree, I saw Pauly running back. Fire engulfed the motorcycles. I never heard him shoot.

As Norm spoke, I began to hear his muted voice. I tried hard to understand him. Rubbing outside my earlobes helped and felt good. He wanted to know if I was okay. I nodded.

The cabin's front door opened and more grenades came out. I don't know if they exploded or not, but they began to emit thick smoke before we could react.

"Smoke grenades," I heard Norm's faint voice.

The misting drizzle helped the dense smoke stay in place. The men inside the cabin planned to make a run into the safety of the woods or down the road.

Norm and Bob fired into the smoke. They must have

heard the men come outside. The smoke hid the cabin from my sight. Pauly picked up the automatic rifle, shot into the smoke and emptied the magazine in a few seconds. Then he took his M4 and continued shooting.

I heard the men standing close to me shooting but it sounded as if it came from a distance. When I stood, I noticed that my jacket bled. I looked down and blood oozed from my pant legs. Where was my M4?

Norm put his arm around my waist. "You're bleeding."

I had cotton in my ears and rubbed them, hoping to make it go away.

"Yeah." I raised my arm so we could both see the blood. "Where's my M4?"

Norm pointed to the edge of the clearing.

"I don't feel anything," I said.

"You will," Norm said. "We need to get you back to the boat."

I shook my head. "Morgan."

As the smoke cleared, the motorcycles burned with an occasional gas tank erupting, sending flames up the wet oak logs of the cabin's wall.

Two bodies lay apart in the mud. That left four, but they may have tried going out the other door and met Parks' shooters.

Pauly came over and I heard him tell Norm that Morgan made it into the woods.

"Where?" I yelled so I could hear myself.

Pauly looked at Norm.

"Where?" I demanded.

Pauly pointed toward the woods on the roadside of the cabin. I saw a blue blur move between the trees. Forgetting the bleeding, I pulled away, grabbed the shotgun from against a tree where Pauly had put it and headed toward the blue blur.

Adrenaline rushed through me as I ran toward the brush,

into the forest with only the thought of capturing Morgan in my head. The muddy ground and slippery leaves kept my pace down. I didn't feel pain from my injuries, yet. With Morgan's size and weight, the slippery ground-covering and muddy patches slowed him as well. I could see he had problems with his footing as he moved.

It was eerie to run through a quiet forest that I knew held many sounds within. I listened for signs of Morgan's movements but barely heard myself as I pushed through underbrush. The blue denim uniform of the Rattlers kept moving in front of me.

As bad off as I was, Morgan's life of partying on Duval Street had him slowing down and huffing after a few minutes, I began to gain on him. Low branches cut me in places I hadn't bled from, especially my face. Stones and roots grabbed at my sneakers and I almost fell a number of times. I probably should have, but I focused on the blue blur and as I moved closer, it only energized me. I said a silent prayer to Robin.

The oak and pine trees grew dense and rain turned from mist to a steady downpour. It slowed us both, but the promise of dimness and a thickening forest worked in Morgan's favor. I brought the shotgun up to my shoulder as I moved along. When I was ready, I stopped, aimed the shotgun and hoped Pauly hadn't used all five shells. I pulled the trigger and flames shot out. Even though the blast seemed muted to me, it caused Morgan to stop and turn. He fell to the ground as he saw the flames coming. He didn't know they wouldn't carry that far. I did and I started moving toward him.

Morgan couldn't have been more than thirty feet ahead of me when he picked himself up. He looked surprised when he saw me. As he turned to run, I stopped again, took my Sig from its holster, and shot at his legs. He fell against an oak. I almost laughed to myself because hitting Morgan at that distance in the downpour was the Hail Mary of shots for me.

Morgan turned and aimed his rifle, as I ran forward. It didn't fire. Maybe he'd emptied the magazine while running from the cabin or it misfired. I didn't really care. I'd broken the Mick Murphy's Law curse. My pace slowed. The shotgun hung from my shoulder as I aimed the Sig at him.

He leaned his back against the oak. Morgan made the tree trunk look thin and weak. He laughed. As I got closer. I faintly heard it.

"Fuck, Murphy, we thought you were the law." He moaned when he tried to move his legs. "What are you doin' here?"

Rain fell on both of us.

Surprise came and then realization followed. "It's the bitch, ain't it? Her white knight, Mick Murphy. Shit, I shoulda let you have her?" He watched my expression. He inched up but his leg wouldn't have it. Years of being a bar bouncer had taught him to read his adversaries.

"Why?" I kept the Sig pointed at him, my finger tapping out the tune in my head.

"Fuck, why?" The shot leg caused him pain he tried to hide. Rain dampened his face. "She was leavin' me. And for what? You?"

A heavy cold rain poured down on us. Morgan kept wiping it from his eyes. I ignored it, having spent most of the afternoon soaked.

"Because you're an abusive asshole!" I shouted. His stupidity angered me. His words tore at me.

"Yeah, well she got what she deserved! And it don't make no difference. Hell, for all I know she was havin' your kid. Damn sure it wasn't mine."

I held in my anger though it boiled inside. "You're going to prison, asshole. Two murder charges. I'm taking you in."

"Murphy, look at your fuckin' self." His smile didn't hide his pain. "You're bleedin' out. You ain't doin' nothin' to anyone."

"Look down, Morgan, you're bleeding out." I pointed to his damaged leg.

He looked down, shook his head in disbelief and tried to hide the pain. "Anyway, asshole, the Rattlers have the best defense attorneys money can buy and I've talked to one in Daytona." He grinned, proud to be showing me how wrong I was. He wiped at the rain in his eyes or, I hoped, it was tears from pain. "There's nothing but circumstantial evidence connecting me to Robin's death. He's already talking to the DA and making arrangements for me to turn myself in."

"No way." I needed to sit down but didn't.

"There's a way motherfucker," he sneered as he wiped at the rain. "Two days in jail, a bail hearing and probably no trial. Now it'll be hospital time, not jail, thanks to you."

"She told the paramedics you beat her." I had to do something before I fell down.

"No, see they got it wrong." He grinned, his face wet and shiny. "She was asking for me! Get it, shithead? She was asking for me, not accusing me!"

Norm and Pauly grabbed me under my arms.

"Jesus, Pauly, you keep bad company," Morgan managed to say, his hand finally reaching down and touching his bleeding leg. "You'd better get Murphy some medical care. He's bleedin' out."

"I'm not dying before you," I said surprised at how weak my voice sounded.

"Perfect justice Murphy, you and the bitch dying and me walkin'."

"You don't care about the baby? Are you that sick of an animal?" I spoke slowly trying to say each word carefully, my anger overriding everything else.

"One less bastard in the world, Murphy," he said.

"Let him be, Mick, the cops will be here in a few minutes." Norm held tightly onto me. "There's a murder warrant for him. He's not going anywhere." Norm took the Sig from my hand.

Morgan laughed. Even with my hearing difficulty, I could tell it was to hide the pain and forced. The gunshot wound had to be hurting.

"He's gonna walk, Norm," I said.

"Then you can kill him." Norm looked at Morgan as he said it. "I'll help."

"When I tell the attorney about you three hunting me down, shootin' me, I think you'll be doin' time, not me." Morgan pushed himself tighter against the tree. "How many people dead out there? Explain that to the law."

He didn't know about the FBI involvement. I wasn't about to tell him.

"Let's go, Mick, you need a doctor," Norm said. "If he walks from the trial, he's a dead man."

"You've told me not to put off what should be done today?" I pushed Norm's hand away with what little strength I could muster. He could've stopped me. I leveled the shotgun at Morgan. Padre Thomas' angels could decide. Did Pauly shoot four times? Had I shot the last Dragon's Breath to slow Morgan? Or was there one more shell in the chamber?

When Morgan realized I might shoot, fear froze his face. "No!"

Too little and way too late.

I lowered the barrel and his face unfroze.

I aimed at his legs and pulled the trigger. Flames shot out, engulfing Morgan's torso. His legs took the impact of the shot, but flames moved up his large chest. He screamed. He tried to stand, but couldn't. His screams continued as he fell to the ground and twisted like a snake in the grass, slithering back and forth.

Norm grabbed me. Pauly had never let go. We turned and walked away. Morgan writhed on the ground. The faintness of his screams, music to my ears. The rain had stopped. I looked toward a patch of blue between the clouds and mouthed, *promise kept, Robin.*

Then my world went dark.

Welcome Back From Where?
Chapter FORTY-SIX

Norm and Pauly raised my arms around their shoulders and carried me as Morgan burned. I am not sure how, maybe I was outside my body, but I watched Morgan slither and scream. I saw Satan pull Morgan's flaming soul from his body and disappear into the Netherworld. It made me smile.

Maybe it was a dream of my unconscious mind. Many things weren't clear to me. I saw Padre Thomas standing by my feet, rosary beads in hand. I wanted to ask him why the angels let this happen, but words wouldn't come. Images came in flashes and were gone before I could make sense of them.

Norm, Bob, Burt, Pauly and Texas Rich stood over me at one time or another, moved about, bitching to Decker to go faster. Norm never got off his cell phone.

Pain didn't settle in until men in helmets tied me down. Loud noise pounded in my head and everything shook. Norm sat above me, wearing headphones, looking as if he'd lost his best friend. I had too much pain to say anything to him. He held his cell phone, looking at its screen. I wanted the pain to go away. My body felt as if it were on fire. Did the devil want my soul too?

I lay on a gurney, the pain and burning gone, feeling nothing as someone wheeled me down a corridor. The only thing movies and TV ever get right is the three-second point-of-view camera angle of ceiling tiles and fluorescent lighting fixtures a patient sees as the gurney moves down a hospital hallway. What a strange thought to have.

Bright white light filled wherever I was. It reminded me of the stories people tell who have died and came back. White light. God. Voices. Peace. I heard voices.

Blackness engulfed me. Left me confused. Had God

condemned me? Had I gone blind? I realized my eyes worked and I was seeing a dense nothingness. It surrounded me. Below there was no floor, above no ceiling. Only a thick, pliable blackness existed. Had I died? Was I to spend eternity mired in the nothingness? I walked, but never arrived anywhere. Never saw anything but nothingness. I didn't panic. My curiosity had me reach out and touch the nothingness. Kick at it, bite it. Why didn't I fall through it?

Nothingness was nothing and yet everything. The last thought I remember having was the discovery that at no time did I feel peace. Everyone who wrote a book or did the talk shows after returning from the dead, talked about the peace they felt. I felt nothing! I became one with nothingness. I wasn't going back!

* * *

Pain stabbed at my head. The nothingness had lightened, turned from black to gray and music entered it. My arms moved and I felt the weight of my body. Had I moved through the nothingness to the other side?

When I opened my eyes, a fog greeted me, replacing the nothingness. I couldn't focus. Someone stood over me. A woman came into focus, briefly, and blurred.

"Welcome back Mick Murphy," the soft female voice said.

I tried to fix on her image, make it clear. *Welcome back from where?*

Soft flute sounds filled the background. I knew the music. James Galway.

My expression must have alerted the woman to my confusion. "You're home, Murphy," she said softly. "Do you need something for pain?"

Her image came in and out of focus. I wanted it to stay in.

"My head hurts." My words sounded mumbled.

"That the only thing that hurts?"

I nodded slowly.

"Your bulletproof vest helped save your life. Do you know what happened?" She sounded like a cop.

Instinctively, I said no. I wasn't thinking clearly, but I knew I needed to protect others, whoever they were.

"Do you remember me?"

I tried to focus, to recall the voice. I shook my head.

"Do you know what day it is?"

Wednesday. The cabin. The forest. Morgan. It happened late Wednesday, I knew that. "Friday?"

"Sunday," she said. "Are you hungry?"

"Should I be?" I didn't know the answer to that either. *How could it be Sunday?*

She laughed softly as if trying not to. "You haven't eaten solid food for four days. I'd be hungry."

Without asking, she helped me sit up. I didn't think about it, I let her.

"Still blurry?"

"Will it go away?"

"In time Murphy."

Galway's flute got lively and it made me smile. He played with the Chieftains now.

"Something funny?"

"I like the music."

She began to touch me, from my legs to my shoulders. More probing than feeling.

"Any of this hurt?"

"I wouldn't call it painful."

"But it hurts?"

"I can feel your touch."

"No burning? You haven't pulled away."

"I guess it doesn't hurt, then."

"I can't stay here forever, Murphy." She'd finished with touching. "I need you up and eating something. The young lady will help you."

"A nurse?"

"I assume a friend."

"You're a doctor?"

"Can't women be doctors, Murphy?"

Things began to come back to me. Old things, new things. "Dr. Carpino!" I surprised myself as the words came out.

"Arianna. We should be on a first-name basis."

"You call me Murphy."

"Doesn't everyone?"

As I laughed, she came into focus. Still blurry around the edges, I recognized her. I couldn't hide my confusion from her, or from myself. How'd I get from the Ocala National Forest to Key West?

"What do you remember?"

I told her about Satan taking Morgan's soul, about my spotty dreams and the nothingness.

"Interesting," she said after I'd finished. "Norm got you away on a boat to where a helicopter was able to pick you up." Arianna began to explain. "You were bleeding out but the makeshift bandages you were wrapped in slowed the bleeding."

"I don't remember any of that."

"You and Norm took a JSOC chopper to the VA hospital in Tampa."

"I'm not a veteran." I had no idea why that mattered or why I told her.

"One does not argue with Admiral Bolter." She smiled. "And he thinks a lot of Norm and even likes you."

"How'd I get from Tampa to home?"

"Thank the admiral again. You, Norm and I came in his jet to the Naval Air Station here."

I knew I owed Norm a major apology for the things I said in Daytona. I hoped he hadn't left the island.

"Where's Norm?"

Arianna checked her wristwatch. "Norm and Nora are

bringing lunch back for Peggy and me. The young woman who has helped me take care of you," she said. "She and Nora were here when we arrived."

"Peggy! Nora's sister."

"Yes and not squeamish, I can tell you that." She smiled.

I heard Norm come into the house and that's when I realized my hearing had returned. Arianna called him to the room. Norm stood in the doorway looking tired.

"Welcome back, hoss," he drawled. "Food in the kitchen."

"Soup for him?"

"Chicken soup from *El Mocho*," Norm said.

El Mocho on Stock Island, a small family-owned restaurant, served some of the best Cuban food in the Keys and I often enjoyed lunch or dinner there.

"He needs to eat."

"Is he decent?"

"Pajama bottoms."

"Let me get a T-shirt on him and I'll walk him to the kitchen."

Padre Thomas stood quietly at the doorway, rosary beads in his hands.

"Next time we meet, Murphy, I want it to be in a restaurant or even the popcorn line at the movies. Understand?" Arianna walked out of the room.

"Yes ma'am." Norm pulled the blankets from me and held my old James Dean T-shirt with the saying, *Dream as if you'll live forever, live as if you'll die today*. He helped me put it on. Did he just find the shirt or did he want to remind me of something? As Norm helped me get the T-shirt on, I wanted to tell Arianna that the pain had returned.

Padre Thomas had gone.

Gentler than I thought Norm could be, he moved my legs to the side of the bed.

"Hold on to me," he said. "See about your balance."

I stood up and my legs wanted to bend but I held onto Norm's arm.

"I'm sorry for what I said in Daytona." I spoke softly, afraid to hear my own voice.

"Of course you are." He laughed. "But who remembers Daytona?"

We walked, well maybe I shuffled out of the room.

"Where's Padre Thomas?" I looked around the empty living room. Appetizing flavors wafted in from the kitchen.

"Haven't seen him in days." Norm held firmly onto my arm. "He was upset I wouldn't let him come on the chopper."

"I thought I just saw him in the doorway."

Norm looked around the room. "Not here, unless he came in behind me."

I needed to ask Arianna what meds she had me on. They apparently caused me to hallucinate.

You Felt the Devil Pull on Your Soul
Chapter FORTY-SEVEN

With Norm's help, I made it to the kitchen table, hobbling not walking, and sat. My body felt like a pincushion, small aches and pains throughout. Nora smiled. Peggy cut up the chicken and potato from my soup into small edible pieces. Plates of chicken, rice, and plantains were on the table for the others. Exciting aromas filled the room. Norm sat across from Nora, Arianna across from me and Peggy sat in the center, after giving me my bowl of chicken soup.

I spooned in a few mouthfuls. The warm liquid felt good, even the small pieces of meat and potato tasted great. After I'd eaten half the bowl, I felt full. In the past, lunch at *El Mocho* included the bowl of chicken soup and *arroz con pollo*. I always finished both and now I couldn't finish the soup.

"Don't force yourself to eat," Arianna said.

I smiled at her, afraid my voice would crack in despair if I spoke.

"Until you feel better and eat a whole meal, you'll also be tired," she said. "Nap." She turned to Peggy. "You'll take care of him, right? See he eats and behaves."

"Yes," Peggy said. "Nora and I will."

"I've got to go back to Tampa, Murphy." Arianna stood up. "If you don't listen to Peggy and she has to call me, I'm sending you to the VA in Miami. Understand? I'm not coming back to Key West."

I nodded and looked at Norm.

"You're on your own with this one, hoss." Norm walked Arianna to the door. I heard them whisper but couldn't understand a word.

Peggy helped me stand. I said a soft thank you. Norm walked me back to my room, when Arianna had gone and when I lay my head on the pillow, I fell asleep. I forgot I had so much to talk to Norm about.

* * *

Padre Thomas stood next to the bed when I opened my eyes. Sunlight peeked through the half-closed door to the living room. He smiled, still fingering the rosary beads.

"You shouldn't worry, Mick," he whispered.

I tried to sit up. Padre Thomas helped me.

"What? Me worry?" I leaned against the pillow, my body still felt like a pincushion.

"I knew you would be okay." He looked tired and sad.

"I wouldn't call this okay, Padre."

"You couldn't die, the angels promised me."

"Some things are worse than death. Fortunately, my condition isn't one of them."

Padre Thomas forced a smile. "Maybe it was a test, Mick?"

"I'm guessing I didn't pass."

He shook his head. "No, you did not."

"Now what?" I surprised myself by believing the angels, real or not, had anything to do with my condition.

"They are disappointed you murdered Morgan."

That comment worried me. Only Norm and Pauly knew that. Maybe they discussed it on the boat ride to the chopper. Would they have in front of Decker?

"Satan has Morgan," I said.

"Yes and he wanted you, too. You felt the heat as he pulled on your soul, didn't you?"

This had to be another one of my dreams. "Padre, what is it you want from me?"

"Mick, you know the parable Jesus told about the shepherd that left his flock looking for a lost sheep?"

I nodded and wondered when I'd wake up.

"The angels want you back in the flock, Mick." Padre

Thomas' eyes opened wide as he spoke. "That's part of my calling. To save you."

"I rid the world of an evil, Padre. Morgan caused suffering and death. He deserved to die and I would do it again, if I had to. Others will live now. Maybe I'm God's avenging angel. Ever thought of that?"

"Mick, you're trying to justify your actions, make them acceptable in your eyes. God has forgiven you. Can you forgive yourself? Norm told you years ago, there's no going back when you cross that line. You've crossed it."

"I have nothing to forgive myself for, Padre. How can you care about a man that beat a woman to death and killed her unborn baby?" In the past, Padre Thomas had said things that didn't make sense to me, but this time he had crossed the line, defending Morgan. Turning the other cheek isn't always the answer.

"I care about you, Mick, we all do." Padre Thomas turned and walked away.

* * *

Peggy pulled at my ear, about the only part of my body that didn't twinge with various levels of pain. When I opened my eyes, Padre Thomas had gone.

"You're sitting up." Peggy fluffed my pillow. "You okay like that?"

"Yeah. Padre Thomas helped me up."

She gave me a doubtful smirk. "When? I didn't see him?"

"Earlier I guess." Sun still shined in the living room.

"I didn't hear him come in," she said.

"Did you hear him leave?"

She shook her head. "We need to talk."

"I think you've got a captive audience. Talk away."

"It's personal." She hesitated when I didn't answer. "Norm kind of told Nora and me about the house."

"The fire?" I knew that wasn't it.

She shook her head again. "I know how you got the house and . . ." She hesitated. "I mean, I'll understand if you want Nora and me to leave."

Peggy offered a half smile. I looked at her face, the cute pug nose, bright eyes, shoulder length dark-brown hair with blonde highlights and thought how glad I felt she'd been there when I arrived, even if I didn't realize it until I woke up.

"The old house pretty much burnt up last year." I took her hand. "The fire served as an exorcism of my past demons, even the good ones I let haunt me."

"Norm told us about the fire." She held my hand firmly. "Maybe you should be in the master bedroom and Nora and I in here. You're going to need to be close to the bathroom."

She made me think for a minute, but some things weren't about to happen. "Maybe tomorrow. But for now, I want you to stay there."

"Nora too?"

"I have a feeling Norm wants her to stay, so yes, Nora too."

Peggy kissed my forehead. "Would you like to try to walk to the back porch? Do it without falling and I'll give you a Guinness."

"Arianna said I could drink?"

"No." Peggy smiled. "Guinness has a lot of iron and iron's good for your blood. But only one."

"Cigar too?" I began to feel better.

"I've hidden the cigars." Peggy helped me off the bed. "The ones Norm didn't share with your friends, anyway."

* * *

Peggy and I sat on the back porch. She gave me one Guinness. I'm not too sure I could've finished a second one, but I wanted to try. I spoke softly at first, not sure how my voice would hold up. Wondering how I really felt about

Peggy and her sister staying in Tita's house. Letting go is not always easy, even when it's right and necessary.

The doorbell rang. It must have been a stranger, because no one I knew ever did anything but walk in. If no one answered, everyone seemed to know where the door key hid on the back porch. Jehovah Witnesses, late on a Sunday afternoon? Peggy got up to answer it.

"Whatever they're selling, tell 'em we don't want any. Tell 'em you're a Catholic. That'll scare them away!"

Peggy gave me another one of her inviting smiles as she left. My smile back lacked her warmth.

Peggy laughed as she returned. "Mr. Popularity, four attractive young women, one with a cute southern drawl, wants to see you." She made a show of motioning for them to enter from the kitchen door.

Dixie led the way, looking worried and nervous but on seeing me sitting she broke into a laugh.

"Thought y'all would look like death, darlin'." She bent down and kissed me on the lips. "You know the girls."

Vicky Evans, Sue Taylor and Sheryl Megan lined up behind Dixie. I knew them from the Slipper. They looked different with clothes on. Maybe even more attractive in a girl-I-wanna-date kind of way.

"Thanks for stopping by." I introduced them to Peggy who brought them each a soft drink.

The women sat around, Dixie leaning on the railing. I sensed they'd rather have a cold beer.

"What brings you by?" I wondered what they'd heard about Morgan.

The women all looked toward Dixie.

"You haven't heard?" Dixie sipped the soda.

"Dixie, you could fill a Walmart with the things I haven't heard."

"The Slipper burnt down." A smile came, not a frown. "We're all out of work."

I looked at the other women, none frowned.

Dixie told me how the Russians had convinced the old man who owned the property to let them manage the club. She said the blackmailing was to continue without having to give Morgan his cut. They brought a few more dancers in.

"They torched the place?" Seemed likely but not if the blackmailing continued.

"Accident," Vicky said.

"Has to be torn down." Sue smiled.

"One less gentleman's club on Duval," Sheryl said.

I looked toward Dixie. "What happened?"

"We sought Chuck's help," Dixie said, talking about the old manager Chuck Meier. "Then a few nights later the club closed and around six in the morning the fire started. Girls upstairs got out okay. But all they had were the clothes on their backs."

"Arson?" I laughed.

Peggy couldn't see anything funny in arson.

"Wouldn't know," Vicky and Dixie said together and laughed.

"What about work?"

"Funny you should ask," Dixie said. "I'm the bartender-night manager at a new bar just opened on Greene Street, The Hangout."

"I'm going to be a bartender-manager at an Irish pub in Cranford, New Jersey, Kilkenny House," Vicky said. "Leaving tomorrow."

"I've got a job as a physical therapist in Connecticut," Sue said. "Figured it was time to use my degree. Less money, but a medical plan."

I looked at Sheryl.

"Don't laugh," she said.

"It hurts too much when I laugh," I said.

"I'm going to work training police dogs in Broward. I used to work in a vet's office before and helped train dogs," she said. "I leave tomorrow, too."

"We wanted to see you before we split up," Dixie said.

"What about the Russians?"

"What about them?" Dixie grinned. "They've got no reason to come back to Key West. In fact, I wouldn't be surprised if the cops wanted to talk to them about the fire. Kind of funny, if you ask me. They lease the place and it burns down." She winked at me.

"Suspicious." I agreed. "I'm glad you're all okay and moving on."

Dixie looked at Peggy, smiled and bent down to kiss me good-bye. "Thanks for killing the bastard," she whispered in my ear.

"Not sure what you mean." We both smiled and they walked out.

Just Like Old Times
Chapter FORTY-EIGHT

When Peggy came back from walking the women out, I had decided not to tell her what Dixie whispered to me. I'm not sure she'd understand my reasoning and didn't want her running away from a delusional man who killed in cold blood, saw Satan and sometimes believed in angels.

"Tired?" Peggy asked from the doorway.

"What time is it?"

"Four."

"Where are Nora and Norm?"

"Nora has convinced Da that Key West would be a good place for a pub." She sat next to me and took my hand. "Norm and she are at a property with a Realtor."

"Really, another pub in Key West?"

"I think it has to do with Norm being here more often and . . . well, you know."

"Norm hates Key West, anywhere hot. And I don't think Nora cools him down!"

"Not what he tells us." She stood up. "I'll make something for dinner."

"I have a little soup left." I stood without help. "You know what, I have a craving for cabbage and potatoes. Any in the fridge?"

"Is Saint Patrick Irish?" she joked, following me as I staggered into the house.

"Actually, he isn't."

"I know." Her laughter carried with it a kindness I hadn't heard or felt in a long time. "Aye, cabbage and potatoes, Irish rice and beans!"

* * *

Norm shook me lightly. The room smelled of boiled

221

cabbage and ham.

"You wanna get up?" Norm stood back. "Peggy's cookin' ham and cabbage."

"Where'd the ham come from?" I had napped on top of the covers. Slowly, I moved off the bed. Norm didn't offer to help. I appreciated that. Holding the headboard, I stood, slipped into my flip-flops and hobbled to the kitchen.

"She called Nora and we picked it up." Norm stayed close. "We need to talk, Mick."

"On the porch."

Peggy and Nora smiled hellos as we walked through the kitchen. The table had settings for four. I thought of home as I inhaled the aromas coming from the large pot on the stove.

"Smells like my childhood in here," I said.

"No men in the kitchen till food's on the table." Nora handed Norm a Guinness and looked at Peggy.

"One," she said and turned to me. "Finish it and you will have water with dinner." I heard the hint of her brogue and took her words as a warning.

I sat down on the porch couch, Norm leaned against the railing. He took a cigar out of his shirt pocket and prepared it.

"That one of my Cubans?" In my mind, I could already smell the aroma.

"Yeah." He rolled it around in his hand before lighting it. "Tasted better when they were illegal."

"You got one for me?" I wanted him to blow the smoke at me. Instead he turned his head sideways and let it flow into the yard. "Me," he pointed the cigar at me, "I'd give you one. What Arianna said, that wouldn't matter." He dragged on the cigar and blew out smoke. "Those two in there threatened me if I gave you one."

We both laughed.

"You ready?" He wanted to brief me on what happened, fill in my blanks. We'd done this before.

I repeated what Arianna had told me.

"You remember shooting Morgan?" More thick smoke sent into the yard.

I nodded. "You and Pauly had me. And Morgan spewed some shit about walking away from Robin's murder. Ah, Norm, any rule against blowing some of that smoke in this direction?"

He blew smoke toward me only to have the soft wind carry it away.

"I guess the angels don't want you smokin' either!" He laughed. "Yeah, Morgan pissed you off and then you shot him. I would've done the same." He drank beer and smoked. "Padre Thomas is probably still mad because I wouldn't let him get on the chopper with us."

"He came to visit. Didn't mention it."

Norm looked surprised. "Really, no one has seen him since we came back and I know he got back because he drove in the Jeep with Pauly."

"You put those two together for that long ride?"

"No, hoss. I was too busy keeping you stuck together. Chopper picked us up near DeLand. But let's go back to the inlet."

Norm told me he and Pauly carried me to the boat where Decker wrapped the more serious wounds and slowed the bleeding. Pieces of shrapnel penetrated my vest. Vests weren't made to stop sharp objects like knives and shrapnel, Norm explained. I was lucky. Everyone, but Padre Thomas thought I'd bleed out before the boat got us to DeLand and the chopper.

Parks called in more backup from the FBI and took credit for everything, leaving us out of it. Norm told them where to find Morgan. We left seconds before local cops and Highway Patrol showed up, then fire engines and paramedics. All the bad guys at the cabin were dead, but two of the three bikers guarding the road lived and spilled their guts.

"Why the VA in Tampa?" That had made me curious since Arianna mentioned it.

"Admiral Bolter got you in there," Norm said. "A quick ride in the chopper."

"I have to thank him for the jet, too."

"Best if nothing is said on any of this. Even Parks was able to keep us out of the reports. He found enough evidence in the cabin and in their storage shed to make Craig and Hubbard forget about us, too."

Norm smoked and drank. Then I knew what seemed off kilter.

"Guinness? Is that Nora's influence? And I hear you love to spend time in Key West! You're under the Leprechaun's spell, *bráthair*."

"I'm not your brother, hoss." Norm knew Irish! "And I don't believe in Leprechauns."

"Better not let them hear you say that! Nora teaching you Irish? Hey, now you can talk to Padre Thomas." I laughed and even got a smile out of Norm. "Did you mention Morgan where Padre Thomas could've overheard?"

Norm shook his head. "Pauly and I never mentioned it."

"Do you think Pauly could've said something on the ride back to Key West?"

"No. If I had to like something about the drug smuggler it would be he knows how to keep his mouth shut."

"Ex-drug smuggler." I always needed to remind him.

"All ex-drug smugglers are either dead or serving a life term," Norm said.

"You're just pissed he never got caught," I said.

"Why are you asking about Padre Thomas?" The smuggler topic died.

"He knew about it. Told me as if he witnessed it. Even the part of Satan."

"Pauly and I weren't paying too much attention to what

you were saying. We were busy trying to get you to medical help."

"Yeah, I know."

Norm laughed. "Well, if you say Satan was there, maybe the angels were too."

"Padre Thomas said Satan came back for my soul but the angels wouldn't let him take it."

"Look it, Mick, you were touch and go, even at the hospital, so he knew that and tossed in his angels to keep you believing."

Nora stuck her head out the door. "Company coming!"

"Who?" Norm said.

"They said make enough for the boat people, whoever or whatever they are."

"Lucky we got the big ham." Norm looked at me.

"Must be Bob and the guys."

"Hell, hoss, you better hope they're coming to see you and not in need of more cigars. Your humidor is almost empty!" Norm blew smoke at me.

"Peggy hid my humidor."

"Get used to it. I think the sisters are here for a while."

"You gonna be the bouncer at their bar, meet Da and all?"

"Nora said I can eat and drink for free! What's not to come back to? Da already loves me and we haven't met. Let the sisters stay here and maybe you'll get close to Peggy . . . who knows? She's a smart kid."

"That's the problem, Norm. She's only a kid."

The front door opened and the bellowing hinted the old times were back.

"What? Maybe ten years younger." He laughed. "She's got a lot on the ball. Give her a chance."

"I'll see how she cooks." I stood up.

"She might not be too young for you, but damn sure you're acting too old for her." Norm went ahead of me into the kitchen. It showed me he knew I could handle myself, even with the pain.

Eight of us couldn't all fit around the table. Pauly and Norm ate leaning against the sink. Texas Rich still had the sling on his left arm. Everyone ate. Peggy gave me a small helping and assured me there was more, if I wanted it. I finished my beer. Pauly handed me a fresh Guinness.

"You're getting a lot of iron." Peggy laughed.

I put catsup on my buttered cabbage and hot mustard on the ham. Peggy and Nora looked on in surprise. Only I had the catsup addiction.

For the first time in a long while, Tita's home felt as if it were really mine. I missed her and my boat, the *Fenian Bastard,* but I enjoyed the crowded kitchen.

Norm leaned over me and took seconds. "Just like old times," he whispered in my ear.

I nodded. "My thoughts exactly." I didn't mention Padre Thomas was missing, but Norm knew that.

THE END

ACKNOWLEDGEMENTS

As always, I owe a debt of gratitude to James Linder for his patience and taking the time to show me the use of small firearms, its limitations and dangers. His expertise, especially with automatic weapons, sniper rifles and shotguns helped me in this writing and any errors with the proper use of firearms are mine.

A thank you goes out to my neighbors Todd Blyth and Cheryl Blyth for walking me through the process and dangers of cooking meth. Their knowledge as peace officers that have dealt with meth labs and addicts helped a lot in this writing. Again, any errors are mine.

Thanks also to my Irish friend Noel Ó'Faoláin for information on bulletproof vests and what they will and will not stop. His knowledge helped me in the writing of the final battle scene. Think I got it right.

I am always grateful to my friends Jim Roberts, Rich Siniscalchi and Bill Murphy for their early reads, suggestions and corrections. Their input is always helpful and appreciated. Well worth the beers it costs me.

Nadja Hansen, my editor, put the final touches on the manuscript and without her it wouldn't read as well as it does.

Jen Musselman has designed another great cover and I thank her for putting up with my constant suggestions and hope she knows I appreciate her talent.

THE AUTHOR

Michael Haskins was born and raised outside Boston, in North Quincy, Massachusetts. His career in journalism began while in high school as the weekend midnight – 8 a.m. office boy in the city room of the Boston Record-American and Sunday Advertiser. He left Boston for a college scholarship in San Juan, Puerto Rico. Politics got in the way and he was back at the newspaper within a year. Soon after he left for Los Angeles where he discovered he didn't have the height or good looks for on-air news. He did join the Greater Los Angeles Press Photographers Association, serving one year on its board and two years as head of its chili cook-offs held at the LA Press Club. He worked at ABC-TV during the prime years of sit coms and variety shows. Twenty years ago, he moved to Key West, Florida to be the business editor/writer for the local rag. Five years later, he joined the city as its public information officer. Once again, five years later, politics interfered and Haskins was out of a job. His book, Chasin' the Wind, was published about that time, 2008. He has freelanced for the bi-weekly Keynoter, been the arts & entertainment writer for the Key West Weekly and been a stringer for Reuters News Service in Miami. Now he writes fulltime and hopes to do two books a year so he can spend his summers in the Irish countryside writing more.

.

43164246R00127

Made in the USA
Lexington, KY
20 July 2015